BOOK 3:

THE BLUE PLANETS WORLD

PILGRIMS

BY

DARCY PATTISON

Mims House, Little Rock, AR

Mims House
1309 Broadway
Little Rock, AR 72202
www.mimshouse.com

Publisher's Note: This is a work of fiction. Names, characters, places, and incidents are a product of the author's imagination. Locales and public names are sometimes used for atmospheric purposes. Any resemblance to actual people, living or dead, or to businesses, companies, events, institutions, or locales is completely coincidental.

Publisher's Cataloging-in-Publication data

Names: Pattison, Darcy, author.
Title: Pilgrims / by Darcy Pattison.
Series: The Blue Planets World.
Description: Description: Little Rock, AR: Mims House, 2017.
Identifiers: ISBN 978-1-62944-069-9 (Hardcover) | 978-1-62944-038-5 (pbk.) 978-1-62944-068-2 (ebook) | LCCN 2017913111
Summary: A small team from Earth travels to Rison to find the cure for a water-borne disease that threatens the Phoke, the mermen and mermaids, of Earth.
Subjects: LCSH Extraterrestrial beings--Fiction. | Mermaids and mermen--Fiction. | Diseases—Fiction. | Interstellar travel--Fiction. | Life on other planets--Fiction. | Refugees--Fiction. | Science fiction. | BISAC JUVENILE FICTION / Science Fiction
Classification: LCC PZ7.P27816 Pi 2017 | DDC [Fic]--dc23

Printed in the United States of America

Other Novels by Darcy Pattison

The Blue Planets World
Envoys, Prequel
Sleepers, Book 1
Sirens, Book 2
Pilgrims, Book 3

Liberty
Longing for Normal
Vagabonds
The Girl, the Gypsy and the Gargoyle
Saucy and Bubba
The Wayfinder

PILGRIMS

And thus ever, by day and night, under the sun and under the stars, climbing the dusty hills and toiling along the weary plains, journeying by land and journeying by sea, coming and going so strangely, to meet and to act and react on one another, move all we restless travelers through the pilgrimage of life. —

Little Dorrit, Charles Dickens

THE PUP

Earth calendar. January 10, 2040

The great white shark moved silently through the warm Risonian ocean, propelled by short sweeps of its crescent tail. It had no conscious thought for what it was doing half-a-galaxy away from its home waters; it just waited. Overhead a gorgeous blue-violet sky reflected a perfect day on the planet Rison of the Turco solar system.

A lone figure emerged from a squat building, trotted down the weathered stone steps to the water, and kicked off sandals. Toes hanging over the edge of the cliff, Utz Seehafer studied the ocean swells ten feet below. When he spotted the shark's fin, he dove, hanging for a moment, a dark form against the brilliant sky. Utz let the dive carry him deep, and then kicked, lazily looking around.

Where was the great white?

A hundred yards away, the great shark heard the splash and stirred, moving toward the disturbance, an arrow shooting toward a bull's-eye. The shark closed in and hurtled past the teen, a dozen feet to the side. Utz's eyes grew accustomed to the underwater filtered light, and his water-breathing through the Risonian gills under his arms came regularly. The villi on his legs had interwoven, or *mokwa*, into a powerful tail.

Utz greeted the fish by flapping his hands to make waves. It was a crude communication, suited only for simple concepts. When the shark answered back a greeting of joy, Utz took off for their usual swim around the enclosure. The female great white used to join him and this mate for a swim, but lately, he hadn't seen much of her.

Utz's dad, Pharomond Seehafer, the leader of the Bo-See Coalition in the southern hemisphere of Rison, had paid smugglers millions for a breeding pair of great whites. They'd been here for a year under Utz's care. He loved the sleek beasts, but really, why were they here? Rison was due to implode within the next few weeks or months, and they wouldn't survive.

Utz realized the great white wasn't following him. Instead, the shark dove, rapidly circling back to herd him downward and toward the opposite shore of the tiny cove. The cove's entrance to the ocean was tightly secured with shark-proof nets. That had been easy because Risonian oceans boasted even more vicious creatures, such as the mighty *kyrra*, than Earth's great white shark. Risonian oceanographers had perfected such enclosures for use in scientific study, and it had been simple to adapt for these Earth creatures.

Utz happily followed the shark, glad that he seemed to have a destination in mind. Kicking lazily, he dove even deeper to where the waters grew murky. Finally, they stopped before a shallow cave. Puzzled, Utz flapped his hands at the shark asking, "What's here?"

The shark ignored him, though, and cautiously nosed into the cave.

In a flurry, the shark backed out and thrust against Utz, shoving him away. Utz barely held his panic in check, almost bolting for the surface. But the shark stopped just as abruptly as it had charged him and turned back to the cave opening. The sleek body quivered. Clearly, he was anticipating something.

Shadows.

Utz peered at the cave opening and swore that something moved. Had some other large marine animal crept into the cove without them knowing?

Another sleek white form burst from the cave.

After an initial shock, Utz sighed in relief. It was just the female great white. She moved to nuzzle the male before darting away with a powerful tail thrust.

Utz turned to go, too, but looked back when he realized the male wasn't following. Instead, he was almost stationary, moving only enough to keep his breathing regular. And he was staring at the cave. Waiting.

Utz let the currents spin him around to face the cave.

Another shadow. Utz half-turned, ready to swim away if needed.

The shadow moved. It was small. White.

Awestruck, Utz froze.

It was a great white pup.

THE CADEE MOON BASE

Jake hugged the wall of the corridors, trying to keep away from the press of people and the babel of various languages. In the last five years, Rison had built ten-story dormitory buildings on the Cadee Moon Base. They could house 5000 comfortably, but at least four times that had crammed into the base, and more desperate individuals arrived daily. Rooms were shared by two or three families. Jake had heard that it was common for families to take shifts sleeping or wandering the halls. When it wasn't your shift, you had to find other places to be. Hence, the crowded hallways.

The medical research team from Earth had arrived at Cadee the day before and spent the time talking with officials, making arrangements to refuel and restock their spaceship, the *Eagle 10*, and other mundane details. They were assigned a suite with two tiny bedrooms and a kitchenette. This was Jake's first time to wander the halls.

Suddenly, someone slapped his back. "Jake Quad-de! I heard you were on the Base, but with this crowd—" A tall teenager gestured toward the mass. "—I didn't think I'd see you."

Surprise gave way to recognition. "Kirkwall Rudak! You've grown, but I'd know you anywhere from your nose ridges."

The boy's nose ridges were thick and pronounced. Jake thought, *Kirkwall will never pass for human.*

"When'd you get here? Did Derry come with you?" Jake said. His Tizzalurian had been rusty at first, but after just 24 hours, he understood everything as if he'd never left. However, he still stumbled when speaking or searching for the right way to say something.

Kirkwall frowned. He was a couple inches taller than Jake and carried himself with grace. "I've been here three weeks. Derry's still down there. She went to Marasca University, and I haven't seen her in several months." Derry was Kirkwall's younger sister. She'd been a grade behind them at school

Jake hesitated, but had to know: "How much did you have to pay to get here?"

Kirkwall's frown turned to a rueful smile. "10,000 yen."

Jake raised an eyebrow and said, "Yen?"

Kirkwall shrugged. "Yen was the preferred payment three weeks ago because the Japanese government said something nice about Rison in some obscure broadcast. The rumor was that they would take 5000 people in Japan. But that rumor was false, and this week, it's India that is supposed to be welcoming us. This week, you'd have to pay in rupees."

"At inflated exchange rates, right?" Jake's voice was tinged with disapproval, but really, what could anyone expect? The planet—the whole, huge planet!—was going to implode soon. When it did, no one would care about Risonian money. They had to exchange everything to some sort of Earth currency and the sooner, the better.

"Derry coming up soon?" She'd always been a cheerful girl, even if she did like her studies too much. On Earth, they would call her a nerd.

Kirkwall looked upward, staring at the ceiling, unable to meet Jake's eyes.

Jake inhaled sharply. "She's not coming? Why?"

"She was caught in a volcanic explosion last year, and it broke her leg. It healed badly. There are strict rules. Only healthy people can evacuate. She limps."

"No!" Jake said. "That's wrong." The tragedy was that he understood. There were so few spots for evacuees that they took any excuse to cross off a person's name. They had to. Millions were going to die, and they could do nothing. But some could live. They had to pick and choose, and it made sense to only bring the strong and healthy.

The whole situation was tragic, partly because it was their own fault. Decades ago, Risonian scientists decided to try to prevent volcanic eruptions by using Brown Matter. No one realized that the Brown Matter would eventually find its way to the center of the planet, and once joined together, the tiny bits became strong enough to create a black hole at the core. It was slowly gaining strength and would one day implode the planet.

Kirkwall's face looked like he was about to implode. He shook his head, as if to shake off the harsh decisions that everyone was making. His voice shook, but he forged ahead. "Anyway, I've been here three weeks. And that's three weeks too long. Your mom making any progress? Will we be evacuated soon?"

His voice carried the same edge as everyone Jake talked with. Tension was building, and these people needed good news soon. Silently, Jake shook his head.

"I know she's trying, but this place is like *ziza* burrows!" Kirkwall said.

Jake grimaced at the comparison. It would be like Dad saying it was like a rabbit warren, which is exactly what Dad had said that morning.

"Where are you going?" Kirkwall asked.

"To Pool #7. We have swimming time scheduled."

The need to swim, to be immersed in water, was like an itch that he couldn't reach. Excitement made his insides quiver. After three weeks en route from Earth, he was almost desperate to swim. Never again would he go months without swimming like they had asked him to do on Bainbridge Island. Did they really think they could stop a Risonian from swimming in Puget Sound? Swimming, water—it wasn't optional for him. It was crucial to his health.

Kirkwall whistled. "I've heard the Earthlings were swimming, and you got a whole hour! All I've had this week is two fifteen-minute time slots. You really are VIP these days. Like your dad."

He means like Swann Quad-de, thought Jake. Living on Earth as just another teenager, he'd almost forgotten what the Quad-de name meant on Rison. He'd forgotten the respect that came with the family name. Coming back to Rison, his biggest fear was facing his step-father again. He'd missed Swann so much. Would he be changed? Would he see and understand how much Jake had changed?

Jake hesitated, then shrugged. "Come with me. We have the pool to ourselves, and no reason why you shouldn't join us."

"Really? Well, sure." Kirkwall's face lit up.

Guiltily, Jake wished he hadn't felt compelled to ask his old friend to come along. The pool would be crowded. But it was the right thing to do.

Kirkwall fell into line behind Jake, and they hugged the corridor walls until they reached the entrance to Pool #7.

Outside the pool, a throng had gathered. A sign pointed up a set of stairs and said, "Viewing Windows." Jake left Kirkwall by the entrance to the pool and climbed the steps to the viewing window. Tiny kids knelt with foreheads or hands on the window. The next row included a large round girl and her skinny friends, all joking about who would win a high dive competition—if they only had a place to hold it. Behind them stood various adults, presumably parents of the kids. The swarm of people were like Earth's bees drawn to a field of sweet nectar, only kept away by a thin pane of glass.

Around the periphery, a dark-haired man stood guard over a woman who was dozing against the wall. He wore a backpack and often called to a scrawny girl, Merry, who knelt on the front row.

Apparently, even if you didn't have pool time, it was entertainment to watch.

Jake stood at the back of the crowd, tall enough to see something of the pool area below. Three lanes were separated by stripes for lap-swimmers. The current swimmers were families. A mother and small boy, maybe three years old, were seated underwater on the pool's floor. Three girls, obviously sisters, ran squealing and cannonballed into the pool, splashing water everywhere. The floors had a slight decline, so the precious water dribbled back into the pool.

"Waste not, want not," Jake could hear his Earth grandmother, Easter, say.

The girls climbed out and got ready to run again. Their parents swam back and forth in lazy circles.

Jake bounced on his toes in excitement. It was a small pool, but it would be enough. Better than what he'd had on the Obama Moon Base, which was a slightly larger than bathtub-sized jet pool, where you swam against a current created by a pump.

In the hallway and in the pool room, a bell rang, and a loud speaker announced, "Five-minute warning. You must be out of the pool and exiting the pool room in five minutes. If you're scheduled to swim next, please line up on the right side of the pool entrance. Allow the others to exit before you enter."

Everything was timed, Jake realized. The man with the backpack sidled up to him. Dark shadows surrounded the man's eyes, and he blinked at Jake and asked, "Are you swimming next?"

Jake glanced at the man and cringed. He looked worn-out. Briefly, Jake wondered how the man had bought his way off-planet. What skills did he have that would be valuable on Earth?

"Yes," Jake said shortly and turned away.

But the man plucked at his sleeve. "Sir, is it true? You get a whole hour to swim?"

Jake narrowed his eyes. Did everyone on this base know his business? "Yes, an hour."

The man put a hand on Jake's arm. "Please. We've been here for 113 days. But we don't have the money for bribes, so we've only been in the pool five times. Still, my Merry, she loves to watch. Please, sir. Could she swim for just fifteen minutes?"

The girl was scrawny, like she wasn't getting enough to eat. From experience, Jake knew the pain of not being allowed to swim. For a Risonian, it was almost torture. And the child—Merry—looked at the water with such longing. Just then, she turned a pleading look to her father. For a moment, she tugged at his heart.

Dad, Dr. Mangot, and Captain Bulmer had arrived and took their place in line. Dr. Mangot and Captain Bulmer were both Phoke, the Mer people of Earth. During the trip from Earth, they'd worn blue camo uniforms with the insignia of the Aberforth Hills Militia from their underwater Phoke city. The group was on Rison to research the water-borne illness caused by the Risonian organism, the *umjaadi*. The emergency medical research team had been assembled in less than a week and arrived here as quickly as possible.

The spaceship from Earth was so, so—he struggled to put it into words—so dry. Desert-like. Parched mouth, parched skin.

He had to swim. But maybe he didn't need a whole hour.

What would Swann do? The old mantra came back so easily. The attitude had been ingrained into him: he should always think of what a Quad-de would do. They served the people and put everyone else's needs above their own.

It didn't matter that on Earth, no one would've given Jake a second thought. He'd be just like this man, who was so poor that he couldn't even buy swim time for his family.

Reluctantly, Jake gave in to the Quad-de directive: "Yes, she can swim with us. Would ten minutes be enough?" He winced inwardly that he'd tried to limit the girl's swim time. "No, no," he said shaking his head at himself. "Fifteen is fine."

"Thank you, sir!" The man's face looked suddenly younger. He crooked a finger at the girl to come to him, and turned to shake his wife awake.

Jake sighed. Would the man heed the time and retrieve her, or would it be a fight to make her leave? If Merry fussed, he'd give in and let her swim the whole hour. And he hated himself for worrying if she swam longer. After all, the pool itself wasn't going to be that crowded with just their group.

When the parents told her that she'd get to swim, Merry crowed with joy and held Jake's hand as they trotted downstairs.

Kirkwall nodded at Merry and said, "What's up?"

"She just wants to swim for fifteen minutes," Jake said.

Kirkwall looked like he wanted to argue, but Jake led the girl past him to the pool. When she jumped into the water, Jake glanced at the viewing window. Her parents were standing at one side and smiling, holding each other's' hands. Jake quickly looked away, embarrassed, as if he'd intruded on a private moment.

Jake dove into the water and sat on the pool's bottom, thinking. This was the problem with coming back to Rison. Here, he was a Quad-de, and the Quad-de were always statesmen. A Quad-de would always sacrifice for the greater good. They were a class set apart. He wanted to be like Swann and always think of others first. Instead, he was half human, and his human half didn't want to sacrifice anything.

Above him, Merry's scrawny legs *mokwa* together, and she swam laps as if her life depended on it. She wasn't wasting a single second of swim time.

Meanwhile, Captain Bulmer and Dr. Mangot swam lazy laps together, pausing often to talk and laugh. During the trip from Earth, they had renewed an old friendship. They'd attended school together, but careers took them different directions. Captain Bulmer was the one most smitten, following Dr. Mangot with his eyes when she wasn't looking. Jake thought Dr. Mangot was too hard-hearted to ever notice. She'd been harsh in her dealings with his family, and as far as he could tell, she never softened.

Merry's father did pick her up at the quarter hour. He bowed to Jake and said, "Thank you, Jake Quad-de. I am Nick Bruce. Your kindness to my Merry Bruce, it won't be forgotten."

Jake nodded, and with perfect manners said, "Just doing what anyone else would do."

Always deflect praise, his mother had ingrained in him.

"No," Nick Bruce said solemnly. "Not everyone would do it. But you're a Quad-de. That's why I was hopeful enough to ask."

Don't put me on a pedestal, Jake thought. *I'm not a real Quad-de.* He was just a test-tube baby who had the good fortune to have Swann as a step-father. On Earth, he'd earned a measure of respect from Mom and Dad. But that was nothing to what was expected of a Quad-de. Jake didn't think he'd ever live up to Swann's reputation or expectations.

THE SMUGGLERS

The *Eagle 10* spaceship was halfway between the Cadee Moon Base and the Killian Spaceport, which was situated on the southern edge of the Tizzalurian Plateau. Jake pressed his nose against the small, thick window, and watched Rison grow larger and larger.

"How long since you've been home?" Dr. Mangot asked. She was pressed against the window beside her seat, engrossed in her first look at Rison. A week before she boarded this spaceship, she hadn't even given Rison a second thought. She was a Phoke. In fact, just a few weeks ago, no one on Earth even knew the Phoke, the mermen and mermaids of the Earth's seas, existed. As a Phoke leader, it'd been a whirlwind month as they announced their presence to the world. As a respected doctor, she'd been busy and happy in her work. Now, she was intently focused on finding the *umjaadi* organism that was causing the Phoke to be sick. It was an impossible task, of course, but one born of desperation.

What will she think of Rison? Jake wondered.

He longed for Em to be here so he could show her the planet. He'd met Em on Bainbridge Island at a coffee shop and had been smitten immediately. Six weeks ago, when she became sick, her birth family stepped in and took her to the Phoke city in the North Sea, Aberforth Hills. Em discovered that her mother was half-Phoke. Em was the first Phoke to be infected by the Risonian *umjaadi* organism. She was the reason Jake was on this medical mission. He had vowed to find a cure for her.

"It's been three years since I've been home," he told Mangot. "I know things have changed, but I'm hoping I can still get some *wolkev* ice cream from the street vendors!"

Mangot grimaced and shook her head. "*Wolkev*! You're a one-track stomach."

"Well, I can find you some nice grilled Risonian bugs-on-a-stick, if you'd rather. Those sell well on the street."

"Ugh!" Dr. Mangot rolled her eyes and returned to her window.

Jake stared at the planet below. His anticipation was like a rising tide that threatened to flood his emotions. He struggled to figure out why he felt overwhelmed. He should be comfortable coming home to Rison, but somehow Earth had changed him. He'd grown up in the last three years, too. That meant he should be old enough to handle this homecoming smoothly.

He thought of David Gordon, his Risonian friend on Earth who was part of a sleeper cell and had never known anything but Earth. David was a natural-born politician and would've been at home in the Quad-de family. Even now, he was preparing to do an internship with Jake's mom, the Risonian Ambassador. If David was here, he'd be calm and prepared to face anything.

Maybe it was the uncertainty that bothered Jake the most. The worry over the planet, combined with the worry about seeing his family after so long—his insides were unsteady, wobbly. The other Earthlings wouldn't understand, not even Dad, who had been to Rison many times. They weren't born on Rison, hadn't lived on Rison all their lives—to them, it was just a watery planet. But to Jake, it was home.

Far below their spaceship, volcanic smoke smudged the clouds, making the atmosphere murky. In a determinedly steady voice, Jake pointed out to Dr. Mangot the Ja-Ram Volcano that glowed red from lava trickling down its sides. He explained that it was perfectly normal. The massive Tizzalurian Plateau was the result of centuries of continuous flow from this volcano.

But then he fell silent. What could he say about the red glow from the other volcanos that spotted the plateau? He counted. Twelve. Fifteen. A couple dozen now, where there used to be just the Ja-Ram. A chill ran down his spine.

Despite the gloomy landscape, his heart beat faster in anticipation because soon he'd see Swann. Jake looked at his size ten boots and his long legs that filled the aisle. He'd grown four inches in the last three years. He ran a hand across his chin and felt the soft stubble. At fourteen—almost fifteen—he'd soon have to start shaving regularly, a gift from his biological Earth father. Most Tizzalurians had smooth faces that didn't require shaving, and beards were rare. Only in the Bo-see Coalition did Risonians have enough facial hair for a beard.

Will Swann even recognize me? Will I be too much like the Earthlings?

Suddenly, the spaceship jerked and stopped.

Jake leaned forward toward the cockpit, straining to hear what was going on.

Dad's voice: "Killian Spaceport, come in."

Then, Captain Bulmer: "I don't understand Risonian. This is the Earth vessel, *Eagle 10*. We carry representatives from Earth. Do you read?"

Jake unbuckled and moved quickly to the cockpit to reach over Captain Bulmer and flip a switch to put the communications on speaker. Captain Bulmer squirmed uncomfortably in the co-pilot's seat. He was tall, over six foot, and the seat wouldn't move far enough back to accommodate his legs.

A voice spoke in Risonian: "Repeat: This is the Fewtrell Freedom Fighters. You will pay a tariff of 10,000 Earth U.S. dollars to land on Rison. We have blocked all your communications with Rison. We are armed and will destroy your vessel unless you comply."

Jake sucked in breath sharply. The Fewtrells were a notorious pirate group based in the Bo-See Coalition, and they regularly claimed responsibility for terrorist acts. But to attack a ship that Earthlings were on? A ship trying to land, trying to come down to a doomed planet?

"Dad, they're smugglers turned opportunists! Everyone expects to pay to leave the planet." He quickly explained the demand and the reputation of the Fewtrells. "But to stop our ship while coming down is an insult!"

Dr. Mangot, who filled the cockpit doorway, raised an eyebrow. "You're outraged that they stop us on the way down, but you consider it normal to pay to leave the planet?"

Mangot's heavy floral perfume made Jake cringe. For the last three days, she'd been trying to smother the overpowering smell created by too many people crammed into too small a space. For Jake, the clash of smells was worse than either alone. He shrugged at her and said, "You should only pay once. It may not make sense to you, but it's normal for us."

"Tell them that we are a diplomatic vessel and carry no weapons," Dad said.

Jake translated the message into Risonian and transmitted, but immediately the Fewtrells responded: "We care nothing for your problems. You'll either transfer the money or we'll shoot you down. Just as you shot down our vessel of peace, the *Fullex*. We are sending the information for the funds transfer. When we confirm your deposit, we'll allow you to land."

The *Fullex* incident meant little to the Earthlings in the crew, but for Jake it loomed as a huge tragedy. 500 Risonians had been evacuating to Earth, despite a ban on their arrival. The European Union shot them out of orbit, killing everyone on board. David Gordon's aunt, had been the lead negotiator and politician aboard the *Fullex*. If the Fewtrells wanted revenge, they had 500 good reasons.

Dr. Mangot said, "How do we know they'll do what they say?"

She was staring through a window at a ship that hung in space beside them. It was a dark metal and looked the worse for wear, with silver slashes in the metal's finish that spoke of battle. Mounted on the exterior were weapons, probably lasers. Their own ship carried no weapons because they were on a diplomatic mission.

With a shrug, Jake said, "We don't know if they'll keep their word. The Fewtrells have a reputation, though. I'd say we should pay."

The vessel didn't look like any Risonian spaceships that Jake had ever seen. There had been rumors, though, about smugglers in the south seas who were secretly building a fleet. Obviously, their fleet was a reality.

Mangot said in a small voice. "Does this happen all the time on Rison? Maybe I'm sorry I left Earth." She was a sturdy woman and looked distinguished in her militia uniform. Her long, thick hair was pulled into a severe bun at the nape of her neck.

Jake ignored her and asked Dad. "Do we have the funds?"

"Not in the Cadee banks," Dad said. "We'd have to transfer from Earth."

"How long?" Jake asked.

"Even with ansibles, communication will take a couple hours," Captain Bulmer said.

Dad nodded with his chin at Jake. "Tell them, we need five hours. And we need ansible communications. They can't block the ansible."

Jake relayed the message and waited.

Silence.

A brilliant flash lit up the cockpit window. Jake rubbed his eyes against the after-vision of Dad and Captain Bulmer's heads in silhouette against the glare.

"What was that?" Mangot yelled.

"We're fine. We're fine," Dad said. "No damage."

Captain Bulmer's face was grim, his mouth tight. He raised a hand to his mouth to chew on a fingernail. "Laser weaponry. They're letting us know that they are serious."

The communications speakers crackled. "You have three hours."

Silence.

Dr. Mangot said the obvious: "They mean business."

Dad was already bent over the ansible, tuning the receivers toward Earth. His normally tanned skin had turned pale during the crossing to Rison. But he'd lifted weights and used the ship's treadmill to run, so he was just as fit as usual. He talked to Jake's mom, Ambassador Dayexi Quad-de, and arranged for the funds to be transferred to an untraceable Swiss account. And no doubt, the money would be immediately transferred to other secret accounts. Then they waited for the terrorists to confirm the money transfer.

Dr. Mangot and Jake returned to their seats to wait. He heard the rumble of Dad and Captain Bulmer talking, but Jake could do nothing. Instead, he glowered at the dark ship in the distance. Swann had to know that the Fewtrells were active, so why hadn't he warned them? These smugglers had nerve, extracting illegal tariffs from a Quad-de! And in U.S. dollars! Had this world gone mad?

Surely Mom had turned around and called Swann on the ansible. Jake doubted Swann could do anything from the surface. They still had to pay the ransom and hope that it really bought them a safe passage. Jake felt a slow rage building, but shoved back the rebellious thoughts. For now, they had to be peacemakers.

In less than an hour, they received the word: "Tariff received. Pleasure doing business with you."

Out the window, Jake saw the dark spaceship drop away and speed toward the southern hemisphere. Bo-See smugglers, for sure, Jake thought bitterly.

Almost immediately, the Killian Spaceport called. They'd received round-about news from Earth's ambassador that *Eagle 10* had been delayed. They were pleased now to welcome the Earth vessel to the Killian Spaceport.

With the crisis over, Jake let himself relax enough to feel the outrage he'd held in check. He no longer wanted to play tourist guide for Dr. Mangot. Instead, he huddled against the bulkhead, forehead against the window, and scowled at the volcanoes that dotted his lands. Dark columns of smoke mixed with white steam clouds, with red fires winking here and there. He barely recognized the landscape.

Rison didn't have much time left.

Those smugglers would get off Rison in their fancy spaceship and would live on Earth as millionaires. They probably charged ten times that amount to leave the planet.

Perhaps this whole medical mission had been doomed from the start. In a world gone crazy, how could they find the *umjaadi* starfish, capture them, and do the medical research necessary to find a cure? But they had to try because Em's life depended on them finding a cure for the *umjaadi* illness. He felt a resolve harden inside, and he sat up straighter. He'd promised Em to find her a cure, and that's what he meant to do. Smugglers or not.

WELCOME HOME

Jake stepped off the *Eagle 10* and searched eagerly for Swann. In Earth's measurements, Swann was six foot ten inches, easy to spot in a crowd.

Nothing.

And then, "Norio!"

Right before him was Norio Tombs. Shorter, maybe five foot ten inches, Norio was a long-time family servant—well, Jake didn't know what to call him in Earth terms. He served the Quad-de family, but he was more like a brother or uncle to Jake. A part of his extended family. A welcome sight!

"Jake! Finally!" Norio said.

The familiar Risonian voice made Jake grin. After so long on Earth, looking only at humans, he was surprised at how Norio's nose ridges made him look alien. Also, his angular face would be abnormal on Earth. Norio stepped forward, and they hugged, clapping each other on the back. A swirl of dust shook loose from Norio's jacket, and Jake sneezed. Norio smelled smoky. It was mid-afternoon, dark and chilly. They would need to borrow warmer clothes. Jake frowned. It was mid-summer in the northern hemisphere. They should be sweating.

Jake looked beyond Norio and raised an eyebrow. "Swann?" Like on Cadee, it was easy to slip back into the Risonian language, like shifting from air breathing to water breathing. It felt so natural and right.

Norio shook his head and grimaced. "Not here. I'm to take you to the estate. He's coming as fast as he can."

Frustration shot through Jake. He'd waited so long to see Swann, he didn't think he could possibly wait another hour. But he must. That thought made Jake's frown slide into a smoldering anger, but he knew that he must slip into the role of a diplomat's child. Work always came first, children second. The good of the country first. Family last. If Mom was bad about this, Swann was the ultimate offender.

"He was here." Norio tried to soothe the old pain. "But when you were delayed, he had other affairs to tend to."

Anger tinged with bitterness threatened to overwhelm Jake. He felt like a pawn in the Earth chess game. Unimportant and someone easily sacrificed.

Jake pushed aside his anger, burying his disappointment as he always had. To his surprise, it was easy to ignore his anger. Maybe the three years away had turned the pain into a dull niggling rather than a sharp throbbing. Or maybe he'd just grown up some and understood Swann's job better. Or maybe he'd slowly boarded up that spot inside that only Swann could hurt. Maybe he no longer gave Swann the permission needed to rip through him emotionally. Thinking about Swann was making his head hurt.

"Swann's not here. Typical of a Quad-de," he muttered to Norio, but without conviction. "OK. Let's go home."

He nodded to the rest of the party, who picked up various bags. Dad carried three bags slung over his shoulders and tilted under the weight of a large suitcase in his right hand. Medical equipment weighed down Dr. Mangot, while Captain Bulmer was left to shoulder Mangot's luggage as well as his own. Even with Norio picking up a load, Jake struggled to balance three suitcases.

"This way," Norio said. He led them to the curb where the Prime Minister's limousine waited. Like Earth's cars, it was a motor-driven vehicle, but it stretched longer and taller to accommodate the typical Risonian.

Dad whistled in appreciation, but Jake just shrugged. He'd never motored across town any other way. They loaded the bags into the limo's luggage area. Jake insisted on sitting in front with Norio. That let the others spread out in back. A window separated the front and back, and that suited Jake. Dad knew some Risonian, which meant that speaking in that language alone couldn't give Jake a private conversation. And Jake had a question for Norio.

"How's Swann? Is he holding up?" He held his breath, worried.

"Things are bad," Norio said. He maneuvered the car out of the spaceport and waved at the city. "And Swann won't leave." His voice was bitter. "Like others, I've served your family for over 30 years, and we expected Swann would reward us by evacuating us early." He shook his head and turned to Jake. "If he wants to stay behind, fine. But don't make us. Will you talk to him?"

Jake squirmed uncomfortably because Norio had never complained about anything. And because this time, Norio was right. Why were the family servants still on the planet? Jake squirmed even more at that thought. By agreeing with Norio, Jake was admitting to himself that Swann was wrong. But the Prime Minister had never been wrong. He was the one person that Jake trusted without reservation. Swann would be taking everything into consideration, even things the servants didn't know about. If the servants were here, it was because Swann had a reason. But what could it be?

"I don't know if he'll listen to me," Jake finally said.

Norio kept his eyes steadily on the road. "Just try. He's a stubborn man, but, well, just try."

Jake nodded. "We'll discuss it. I can't promise anything more."

Turning his attention to the city, Jake was shocked. As they drove slowly across town, people thronged the streets as though everything was normal. Every man, woman, teenager, child, building, vehicle, shrub, walking pet or flying equivalent of Earth's birds was soot-stained. A fine layer of ash lay everywhere like an itchy wool blanket. In places that might not get disturbed, like an alley, the ash was several inches thick, as if there had been an unnatural snowfall. The central food market had piles of vegetables and fruits protected from the ash by plastic sheets. The afternoon theatre had a long line waiting for the box office to open. And the playgrounds were full of screaming and laughing children. Some people wore masks, but most didn't. It seemed to be life as normal, if a bit dirtier than usual.

Norio explained that chaos threatened at every turn, and Swann worked extra hard to make sure everyone was safe from the threat of daily violence. In some countries, governments had collapsed, and it was everyone for him or herself. In Killia, though, daily life continued with dignity in the face of disaster. But not without inflicting great stress on its leader.

The gloomy ride across town deepened Jake's worry. It was one thing to know that volcanoes were everywhere on a planet, but to see throngs of people walking through the ash-filled air while trying to breathe, that was something else.

At the Quad-de estate, servants immediately stepped forward to open the car doors for the team of Earthlings.

Looking up, Jake smiled ruefully. The courtyard was swept clean of all ash, something that must keep three men busy day and night. Swann probably justified it by saying that he was keeping three more families fed. It was life as usual. As if they weren't about to be blown up.

Emotions swelled as Jake looked up at the ancient house. Built about 200 years ago, the Quad-de's mansion was built with locally quarried granite and marble and roofed with slate—all igneous stones, of course. Pale pink granite made up the walls and the arches in the center that led to the interior courtyard.

Norio strode across marble flagstones and threw open the massive ten-foot doors. Looking at Jake, his face vacillated between a smile and a frown before he whispered, "Welcome, home."

Jake's heart swelled with joy. He was home!

On Earth, it had been easy to start to feel like an Earthling. He enjoyed his Earth grandparents, the Earth high school, and Earth friends.

But here, that all melted away. This solid, stone house, hundreds of years old, it was the foundation of his life. Every stone used to build it was igneous. Born of fire. It was Risonian through and through. Like Jake.

"Let me give everyone a tour!" he called happily.

They left their luggage in the car for the staff to sort out and deliver to rooms. Everyone followed Jake, including Norio, on a quick tour of the house. The upper floor, which was on ground level, was living areas: a large gathering room, a well-used library of both digital and print books, a dining room with a massive table, a tiny room of refreshments that were kept replenished all day long—Jake stopped to grab a candied *wolkev* and even remembered to offer one to everyone else—and a huge conference room with a table made in four parts so it could be arranged as diplomats' whims dictated.

The next floor down held the bedrooms, and Norio quickly showed each person his or her assigned room. They continued the tour, though, and when they came out on the bottom floor, they turned left to the kitchen. It served the dining room with trays sent up a shaft on pulleys, rather like a dumb-waiter in the castles that Jake had visited in Scotland.

Excitement pulled at Jake, though, as they went back to the stairs and turned right. He explained to the others: "The estate is on the edge of a cliff face and the house is built partly above water and partly under water."

A long rectangular room was walled on three sides. The last side, though, appeared to be a long rectangular pond with stairs the length of the room that led down into dark water. The fourth wall, which rose above the water, was bare rock. Norio flipped a switch and lights along the edges of the steps suddenly lit up, inviting them to step down into the water. It was like walking down into an amphitheater, except the stage was submerged.

Jake always thought of it the other way, though. When he walked up out of the water, it was like walking onto the stage. Anyplace where Swann sat transformed into a theater. At one end of the room, a thick multi-colored rug set off a large space.

With a twinge of pride, Jake said, "This is Swann's desk."

Swann had other desks and a massive office upstairs. But he liked to be in the middle of the household, in what he called his day-office, to watch who came and went, and to be interrupted all day, to be in the thick of things.

Jake's throat tightened when he saw a framed photo on Swann's desk. Dayexi was laughing up at Swann, who hugged an eight-year-old Jake. It had been his birthday and for once, they'd left town, taking a picnic lunch. They ended up on a cliff overlooking the sea, where they picnicked. Norio had been with them and took this picture. Jake had always kept it in his room, but he hadn't been able to pack many pictures when he evacuated to Earth's moon. He had others of Mom and Swann, but not this one. He vowed to himself that he would take it back to Earth this time. With difficulty, he pulled himself away from the nostalgia of Swann's desk and put on the bright smile of a tour guide.

The marble floors slanted, almost imperceptibly, toward the steps. Jake explained, "When you come up, any drips will slide back into the water."

Captain Bulmer strode to the water's edge, bent, and touched it. He rubbed his fingers together as if he could tell a chemical composition by feel alone. "Warm. Clean." He nodded at Dr. Mangot.

She eyed the water with longing. "I'd love to swim. But not yet. Not till we see how it goes with the diplomats." She nodded to Jake. "I'd like to go to my room and rest."

The others agreed, so Jake went back to the second floor with them and made sure they knew how to find their bedrooms.

Norio said, "I'll help them get settled in. You can go explore."

With a grateful smile, Jake nodded. He slipped downstairs and stepped into a changing room. From a stack of extras, he pulled on a pair of swim shorts. Back out in Swann's day office, he walked down the lighted steps into the water.

Rison. Home.

The water covered him and filled him and soothed him and excited him. For months, he'd longed for these waters and not known it. His water breathing through his gills came easily. Home.

Underwater, the rooms repeated what was above ground: dining room, refreshments room, gathering room, and conference room. They wouldn't use the underwater rooms this week though because of Dad. The Phoke would be fine, but not a human.

Jake lounged on the chairs in the gathering room, not wanting to go up and dress for dinner. He sank into an attractive and comfortable lounge chair made of compressed seaweed and closed his eyes. How many times had he longed to be here? And now, he was here and Swann was not. He closed his eyes to rest for a few minutes.

Jake woke to a familiar sound. He remembered visiting his grandparents, Swann's parents, at their underwater estate. There, his grandparents used an old language to communicate. It wasn't speech, but a series of clicks, whistles, and grunts. Well, it was speech, but not words like English or Spanish or Chinese. Earth's international phonetic symbols couldn't record Risonian sounds. Underwater, vocal chords don't generate sound waves in the same way as they do in air. Instead, ancient Risonian speech was a complicated series of sounds created by clicking teeth, clucking the tongue, and using low-pitch grunts that transmitted well through the water. It was called the Old Speech, and for those who only lived in the seas, it was the only language they knew. And of course, planet wide, there were many dialects. As Risonians colonized dry land, though, they developed speech more like Earth languages. For a thousand years or more, most of Rison spoke Earth-like speech, and Old Speech had become rare. Jake wondered if it was like the mermen changing their name to Phoke. The utility of either name was fine, but Phoke was an updated name that meant you weren't old fashioned.

For Jake, Old Speech was the sound of holidays. Of family storytelling, gossip, and singing.

Someone was calling him, saying, "Jake Quad-de, are you truly home?"

His eyes flew open. "Swann!"

Instantly, he was on his feet and hugging his step-father. He gulped and clung, desperately trying to not cry. His earliest memories were of Swann and Mom, Mom and Swann. He saw the strong, athletic man that Swann had been, battling through strong currents to pull Jake back to the beach where they were vacationing. Jake didn't know why that image came to him out of the swirl of memories, but for a moment he wanted to feel Swann tugging him out of danger to a safer place. He shivered, and the feeling was gone. The ache which remained weakened him for a moment so that Swann really was holding him up. He straightened, sad that he was older now and wasn't allowed to be a child.

Finally, they both stepped back to look.

The dying planet had aged Swann. He was bare-chested and only wore swimming shorts like Jake. His once strong chest and arm muscles appeared shrunken, as if he was self-destructing from within just like this planet.

"Are you OK?" Jake asked carefully. Underwater, his voice didn't carry well, but Swann understood. They could talk, but for a real conversation, they'd need to go up to the air.

Swann said. "Fine. Just tired."

Jake sank back to the lounge chair and pulled Swann to sit beside him. "I'm here now. Let me help."

Swann pulled him into another hug before answering, "No. You have your own mission. I won't let my worries stop you from helping the Phoke find the cure they need."

Jake knew Swann was right; he had to concentrate on the medical mission. For Em's sake, yes, but also for the sake of all Risonians who might or might not be allowed to live on Earth, depending on the results of this mission.

He nodded. But he kept his eyes on Swann's face. "The medical mission is my priority. But I want your promise on one thing. You will escape this planet and not stay behind."

Swann smiled and reached a hand to touch Jake's chin. "You're going to need to shave soon, aren't you?"

Jake understood. He was half Risonian and half Earthling, and Swann was just his step-father. More important, he was the Prime Minister of the largest country on Rison. Their paths were different. Had always been different.

But Norio was right to be concerned. Did the servants have to share Swann's fate? He forced the question out. "Why are the servants still here? I expected Norio to meet me at the Cadee Moon Base."

Swann shook his head slightly, as if confused. "But I'm still on the planet. Why would my servants be on the moon?"

"Because they trust you and expect you to evacuate them in time."

"Oh." Swann's eyes opened wide, startled. "Oh."

"You were going to send them away soon. Right?" Jake pressed.

"No," Swann said simply. "I hadn't even thought about it. I'm so busy—how would I eat if the cooks went off-planet? I wouldn't have clean clothes and the house and gardens—" He trailed off.

"Just don't leave it too late," Jake said softly. He'd already said too much, already caused Swann to criticize himself for wanting his household to be in order as usual, for wanting to cling to the familiarity of normal.

Grimly, Jake said, "Promise me. You will escape."

Swann shook himself, and then stood to pull Jake upright. Swann ran his eyes up and down. "You've grown! How tall?"

Jake glared, wanting to pull the right answers from Swann. Grudgingly, he said, "Five foot, ten inches in Earth's measurements."

"So. Tell me about this young Phoke woman. Em? Is that her name?"

"Emmeline Tullis." Jake knew that Swann was deliberately distracting him from the issue of evacuation. But he also knew that he'd lost the argument because Swann would do his duty—whatever that was. "She's amazing." He'd been wanting to have this conversation about girls with Swann for so long. They strolled back to the stairs, and up into the air. They shook off water. Jake ran a hand down each arm and leg to wipe off extra beads of water. Swann did the same thing. They sat on lounge chairs. Jake took his time telling Swann how he met Em at a coffee shop, how she wanted him to join the swim team—stopping to explain the swimming competitions—and how hard it was to resist.

Swann didn't take his eyes off Jake while he talked. Finally, Swann said, "I have this one piece of advice. Follow your heart." He paused and a sadness stole over him. "I should've followed my heart long ago and maybe things would've been different."

"Are you talking about Mom and—Blake?" Jake was suddenly embarrassed because he'd almost used the name Dad instead of Blake.

Swann shrugged. "And much more. But let's talk of better days."

"Hello?" Dad—no, it was Blake while they were on Rison—stood in the doorway.

"Here," called Swann.

Blake strode forward and shook Swann's hand.

They both look grim, Jake thought. *I wish my dads could be friends.*

Blake's lips were thinned, and he looked ready for a fight. "Why didn't you meet us at the space port?"

Shock at Blake's rudeness made Jake step closer and put a hand on Blake's arm.

Jake shook his head.

Blake pulled his glare from Swann and squinted at Jake. "No," he said. "This is important. He hasn't seen you in three years, and he left the airport before we arrived."

Swann inclined his head and said in a frigid voice. "My son is home."

He emphasized the "son," and Jake saw that it was like a stab at Blake.

"And I'm here to celebrate that," Swann continued. "But I have many duties that pull me in many directions. When you were delayed, it gave me a chance to visit the nearby hospital's burn ward. All our hospitals are full, but especially the burn wards. We never know where a new volcano will form and many people are caught."

"Oh," Blake said and blinked. He was tall, 6'2", but Swann's height made Blake look short. "Still. The fate of your world. . ." He trailed off.

"It looks dismal, doesn't it?" Swann said agreeably, as if he was talking about a weather forecast. "Of course, in the long run, it doesn't matter that I stopped by the hospital. But for those people, for that single moment. . ." He stopped, clenching his fists, and obviously held back a surge of emotion. "Lately, it seems, we only live for today."

Embarrassment flooded Jake. "Blake, drop it!"

Dad wrinkled his forehead and whispered, "You were so disappointed when he wasn't there."

"But I understand."

"That's it," Blake said. "You've always had to understand that you weren't important to him."

Swann's hand flew up in a gesture of warning. "You know nothing, Earthling, of what Dayexi and Jake mean to me." His words were deliberate and slow. "Say no more. Or, I won't be responsible for my actions."

Blake stepped back, and Jake almost felt sorry for him. Swann's threats were legendary in Killia, and Risonians knew that he backed up every one of them. If you forced Swann into a situation where he threatened you, it didn't bode well for you.

Blake was a Navy man, though, trained in evaluating combat situations. And knowing when to retreat.

He turned to Jake and asked lightly, "How do we know when it's time for supper?"

The kitchen, at the other end of the floor, smelled of spicy fish and vegetables, making Jake's stomach rumbled. He hoped there would be *wolkev* pie. "Should be soon," Jake said. "I'll gather everyone when it's ready."

"Then I'll be in my room," Blake said. He turned and trotted up the steps.

Swann murmured, "Wise man. He retreats so he'll live to fight another day."

Jake's heart ached for the two men. His two fathers were the major conflict of his life. His mixed heritage meant he was pulled by conflicting loyalties: the fight floor v. the basketball floor. Bainbridge Island v. Killia. *Wolkevs* v. apples. The office of the Prime Minister v. the duties of a Commander of the U.S. Navy. Respect v. respect. Love v. love.

Jake didn't want either side to win or lose.

Welcome home, he thought wryly.

GODZILLA

Wind whipped the cove's water into white-capped waves.

Utz helped Derry Rudak down the rough slope. A flimsy red scarf flapped around her head. In exasperation, she stopped to tie it tighter. Utz found himself enchanted by this beautiful Tizzalurian. Ebony hair, thick eyebrows and the clearest complexion he'd ever seen gave her a fresh look. He was aware that his own stocky build was a contrast to her slim figure.

Cautiously, Derry stepped forward with her right leg, balanced, then dragged her left leg down to meet the right. She paused to catch her breath, then repeated the steps. The leg brace on the left leg was hidden under her pants, keeping her upright and mobile, but she was far from graceful.

"Take my hand?" Utz offered.

"No!"

Utz groaned to himself. He'd offended her. It was hard to know when to offer help and when to let her tough it out. Reluctantly, he turned toward the water and walked on without looking back.

At the beach, he shed his outer clothes, just leaving on swim shorts. Then he sat staring out at the cove, but noticing nothing. He was nervous about what he had planned.

Derry joined him several minutes later, panting with exertion. She dropped heavily onto a large rock. While she stripped to her own swim suit, she asked, "What's its name?"

"Godzilla," Utz said.

"What?"

"It's an Earth name for an Earth creature. There's a Japanese myth about a huge creature named Godzilla. It goes around smashing things and killing people."

Derry looked sideways at Utz. "You're serious?"

Utz held up a hand, as if taking an oath. "Very serious. Look it up."

He'd spent many days reading up on Earth mythology, and he quite liked the Godzilla stories. He spoke English, the business language of Earth, but he'd also concentrated on Japanese, watching hours of videos from Japanese speakers. He hoped to live in Tokyo—if he ever made it to Earth.

"Will this shark go around smashing things and killing people like its namesake?" she asked.

"No. Of course not," he said with a smirk. "Godzilla is a myth."

Utz walked into the water and turned to watch Derry. She unbuckled the leg brace on her left leg and awkwardly stood. A livid scar meandered down the outer leg. When she'd been caught by debris from a volcano blast three years ago, the bone was crushed. Doctors inserted a medical grade metal rod, but it left her in the brace. They might've done more if the planetary disaster wasn't pending. Utz knew her well enough by now to understand that just plain walking hurt. The pain left her touchy sometimes, but she never complained. He admired her courage in carrying on.

He waited until she stood upright on her good leg, and they dove together. Underwater, her limp disappeared and a natural grace took over. With her legs *mokwa* together, her strong leg could compensate for the weaker.

They could talk underwater, but water carried voices with less efficiency than air, and they sounded like they were whispering. That just meant they had to swim close to each other, which didn't bother Utz at all.

Derry said, "So, you leave tomorrow for Tizzalura to meet the Earthling medical research delegation. Any surprises?"

"I hear that Jake Quad-de is officially part of the Earth delegation now. I met him once, not that he'll remember. My father was in Killia as an ambassador, and I went along. We were invited to watch a fight floor. It must've been right before Jake went off-planet."

"Good or bad?"

Utz laughed in a burble of water. "He studied with some Bo-See knife master, so he was good. For a Tizzalurian. Bad for a Bo-See."

"But what will your father do? Will he allow the Earthlings to come south?"

"I don't know." Utz shook his head. "On one hand, it doesn't matter because the planet will implode soon anyway. But on the other hand, the planet will implode soon, so we should end our days with dignity." He was repeating arguments he'd overheard at his father's table, and he had no idea what his father, King Pharomond Seehafer, would decide.

Derry agreed. "These are dark days and few of us will make it out. That's why a day like this is special."

They were supposed to be at work, but had agreed: they would come out and enjoy the beauty of their planet. Everyone was skipping work, so it didn't matter anyway. The only thing that kept Derry going in was the responsibility of caring for the animals they kept for research. She couldn't let them starve. But after she fed and watered them, she left whenever she liked.

By now, they had swum across the cove and neared the cave where Utz had last seen the great white pup. He hoped the pup would still be there because he wanted Derry to be impressed.

At the cave opening, he stopped and waved her back. Slowly, he let himself drift toward the dark. Something moved. A white form surged from the cave.

The pup had grown! About half the size of the parents, the young great white bared its teeth at Utz and Derry.

Derry backed away, but Utz merely flapped his hands, sending waves toward the shark that said, "Friend."

The shark slowed. For a moment, Utz was sure the shark possessed a great intelligence, and if they could only break the code, they'd be able to communicate. The pup's eyes seemed to understand the word, friend. But his blue eyes darkened to navy, and he turned to dart back inside its cave.

Utz turned to Derry. "Well?"

Her eyes were large, and her hair floated around her face like a dark halo. "That was amazing."

"Derry, I leave this evening."

She looked down. "I know."

Utz desperately wanted to please his father, wanted his father to be proud of him. But his father would never understand what he did next. Officially, he was engaged to Mitzi Adams, the daughter of a politician who supported the Seehafers. But his heart had never been in it.

He took a deep breath through his gills. "If I can find a way to get to Cadee, would you come with me?"

Her face jerked up. Even underwater, a sudden hope made her face glow. "I'm crippled. They won't let me."

Utz knew that her brother, Kirkwall, had already gone up to Cadee, and she was resigned to her fate on Rison. When her brother went off-planet, she'd cried for a week before she straightened her back and insisted that Utz take her on a picnic.

"I want to live on this glorious day," she had told him. "Not whine away for what I'll never have."

She never spoke of her brother again. But it didn't have to be that way.

"If I can find a way," he repeated, "would you come?"

They needed more time, Utz thought. He'd like a year to get to know her better, a couple years to grow up together. But time was running out. Somehow, he had to find a way to get off-planet and take her with him. She was the only one who understood Godzilla, who understood him.

"Yes." Her voice was as soft as the brush of seaweed against his cheek.

He leaned in closer.

"If you can find a way," she said. Then she smiled, her face dimpling. "And if you promise to save Godzilla, too."

"Yeah," he said with a laugh. "I'll save you and Godzilla."

STRATEGIC PLANNING

That evening, after getting settled into their new rooms, the Earthlings—Dr. Mangot, Captain Bulmer, Blake, and Jake—gathered in the dining room on the top floor. Jake introduced Swann, and they all chatted while waiting for dinner to be served.

After a few pleasantries, Blake asked Swann, "You know about the Fewtrell Freedom Fighters?"

"Is that what they are calling themselves?" Swann motioned for the group to move to the table, where he sat at the head and put Jake at the other end.

"You know who they are?" Blake accused Swann.

"Of course. Their leader is Ancel Fallstar, a Bo-See smuggler. He's been a leader among the Bo-See coalition for the last fifteen years. He always was a smart man. I believe they now have five spaceships. Not enough to be a full fleet, but enough to take their piracy to a new level."

"You didn't warn us about them." Blake's voice was accusing.

Servants came around with platters of food, and Jake recognized a couple favorites: *orton* roast (a ham-like meat), steamed *puck* (a sweet and sour broccoli-like vegetable), and *wolkev* pie for dessert.

"It's the first time they stopped a vessel coming down," Swann answered Blake. "Before this, they stopped vessels leaving Rison's atmosphere."

"Why don't you do something about them?"

Swann said, "The situation is worse than you know. Come. Let's eat. After that, we'll go over everything in detail and plan what to do next."

Blake had to agree, for it was Swann's house, and he was Swann's guest. The supper was lengthy and full of questions from everyone else about Risonian culture and customs.

Jake said little. He just watched the Earthlings and wondered how such an important mission could have fallen to them. Earth and Rison were tied together now by ecological issues. The *umjaadi* organism was thriving in Earth's oceans and would inevitably infect the whole Phoke population. If they didn't find a cure soon, Earth wouldn't allow Risonians to evacuate to Earth. They would create hysteria that the *umjaadi* illness could be spread to humans on land, or some other ridiculous gossip. If they stopped the evacuation, the Risonians culture and customs would become extinct. He felt weighted down by the responsibility, as if he'd landed on a large planet with a huge gravitational pull, and his weight was doubled.

As food was served, though, the conversation turned toward lighter things. Jake ate three pieces of *wolkev* pie, almost satisfying his hunger for all things Risonian. They moved to the conference room for coffee, or *verki*, the Risonian equivalent. Technicians arrived with equipment for Jake to translate. He had a miniature microphone on his shirt collar that transmitted to ear buds that were provided for each Earthling. The technicians were followed by a couple Tizzalurian officials who gave them a quick update on the grim situation on Rison. They estimated perhaps a month, maybe two before the planet imploded. If they used every available planet-to-Moon spaceship, they still could only evacuate 500 people a day. The moon base could accommodate much larger transport vessels, so the trips to Earth could accommodate larger numbers. The bottleneck was in getting people from Rison to Cadee.

Jake would have to translate everything for the Earthlings, so he was pleased when the equipment worked well.

After the gloomy forecast, the Risonians asked if the Earthlings had questions.

Blake immediately asked about Dolk's technology, and Jake translated into Risonian: "Have you tried Dolk's technology? Surely his TAG-GIMS—his tungsten anti-gravity gradient-index meta-surface—would make a difference."

One of the Tizzalurians answered, "We tried it. And it does work. It's just far too late for Rison. If we'd known five years ago. . ." He trailed off.

The weight of the planet's fate pulled even harder on Jake's conscience. If only he'd known that Mai-Ron Dolk's technology was secret. If only he hadn't been so weighed down with grief over the loss of his best friend, Stefan. If only he'd mentioned the TAG-GIMS to someone, anyone. If only.

Instead, full of grief when his friend died, Jake hadn't told anyone about Dolk's technology. It only came out a couple months ago when he was trying to stop sabotage on Earth's volcano, Mt. Rainier.

The information was far too late for Rison.

Jake knew Rison's destruction wasn't his fault, but he could've slowed it, maybe stopped it.

If only.

It was ironic how a freak accident—the lightning strike that flipped the Dolk's car killing father and son—had changed the fate of a planet. And tragic how a freak accident—breaking an *umjaadi* globe in Puget Sound—might endanger all the Phoke on Earth. They had to find the cure for the *umjaadi* illness. Em had to live.

Jake turned his attention back to his translation duties.

"Will the Bo-See Coalition allow us access to the southern seas?" Dr. Mangot asked.

"Seehafer is reasonable, but his ministers? No, they won't let you in," grumbled a Tizzalurian official.

Blake said, "If we don't have permission, are there ways to get there anyway? Unwatched areas, places where stealth will get us to the right locations?"

Swann Quad-de stood and paced. He wore his official black uniform with straight legs, a jacket with shiny stones as buttons, and a short cape. He reminded Jake of the lava fields, where black stone covered the surface, but underneath, there bubbled a dangerous flame. "You understand, I can't be a party to stealth." He said the word "stealth" with scorn. "If crazy Earthlings do unexpected things, well, I can't be held responsible."

Nodding, Dad said, "Of course. Any attempt to reach the southern seas on our part would be unauthorized. Plausible deniability."

When that was translated, Swann's nose ridges wrinkled deeply. "I've not heard that term before. A useful bit of language."

Dr. Mangot said, "Then, how long? When can we get there?"

Swann sat in the largest chair and flipped his cape back. "The International Council meets tomorrow. It'll be at least two days of discussions before anything can be decided."

"Two days!" Dr. Mangot exploded. "Too long. We must start traveling by the end of today."

"Must we?" Swann answered innocently in English.

Dr. Mangot swore and said through clenched teeth. "My people are in danger."

Jake understood her frustration. She was used to giving orders in the hospital, and in Aberforth Hills, her orders were instantly obeyed. But she was out of her sphere of influence here and would have to wait for Swann to act. Dr. Mangot wouldn't stand for inactivity for very long before she did something rash.

Dad defused the situation by rising to walk to a window. Though it was full dark, the horizon glowed red. "How many new volcanoes this month?"

"Around the world? Hundreds," Swann said grimly.

"We're playing a dangerous game if we wait. But it'll be faster with cooperation. Three days. After that, we must find an alternative. We've no idea how long it will take Dr. Mangot to find what she needs. And time grows very short." Dad turned back to the group. "Agreed?"

Captain Bulmer, who'd been silent, was the first to say. "Agreed."

Jake nodded. "Agreed."

Dr. Mangot was the last to speak. Her compressed lips and straight back said, "No." But she grudgingly said, "Three days only. Agreed."

"Good," Swann nodded. "Get some sleep and get adjusted to our time zone. The International Council begins at daybreak tomorrow. I'll be busy the rest of the day welcoming guests. Please don't wander the hallways because the Council may not appreciate your presence. For meals and gathering, please use the small dining room on the second floor where your rooms are located. International guests will be housed underwater in our most luxurious rooms, so they won't see you unless you're out and about. Tomorrow, I'll introduce you all together to the Council. I'll send a guard at the proper time to escort you. Understood?"

Dad answered before Dr. Mangot could. "Understood. Till tomorrow then."

Swann nodded and turned to go, followed by his officials and bodyguard.

Jake followed and said, "Sir?"

Swann turned back. "Yes?"

"May I offer my services today? I know the estate and could direct people as you wish, help with luggage, carry things from the kitchen. . ."

Swann put a hand on his shoulder and nodded solemnly. "It might help. Just be sure you're polite to everyone."

"Of course! I'm not a child any longer."

"Have you grown up while you've been on Earth?" Swann ran an eye up and down quickly, evaluating Jake's height. "More than just growing taller?"

Have I grown up? Jake asked himself. Certainly, Mom and Dad had learned not to ignore him or to try to hide things from him. They needed to know what was happening to him, and they needed to understand what he thought about situations. They had learned to respect him. He realized that Swann had no reason to respect him as an adult. He'd have to earn that from Swann, just as he had with Mom and Dad.

"I'm a son of the house of Quad-de, and I'll make you proud," he said formally.

Swann pulled him into a hug, and said in a husky voice. "I'm so glad you're home."

WE ARE RISONIAN

Jake balanced a tray of hors d'oeuvres on his arm and wove through the crowd to the Bo-See Coalition officials. He offered officials the cheese and golden *wolkev*, a special variety of the fruit that only grew on the plateaus above Marasca, Bo-See's capital. Swann had spared no expense to make everyone comfortable. Jake's tray was almost empty when someone stopped in front of him wearing the Bo-See uniform of white robes, white leggings, and white sandals.

"Hello, Jake Quad-de." It was a smooth, deep voice and spoken in Boadan, not Tizzalurian. As part of his training as a Quad-de, Jake was fluent in the language.

Looking up, he saw a younger Bo-See, short and thick. Basically, the Bo-See came in two types: the Seehafers who were broad-shouldered, strong warriors who never took prisoners, and the Boada, who were tall, skinny blood-thirsty sailors. This one took after the Seehafer line, so the Boadan language puzzled him.

"Hello. How do you know me?" Jake said politely in Boadan. He half-turned to let another Bo-See take a piece of golden *wolkev*.

"I watched you once on the fight floor, just before you went off-planet. My name is Utz Seehafer." He stuck out his left hand to shake.

Jake understood instantly: the left hand never carried a knife.

Looking closer, Jake saw that Utz was probably his age, or maybe a year or two older. He shook Utz's hand with his own left hand. "Son of His Highness, Pharomond Seehafer, I assume."

Utz nodded. "How long have you been back? And what's Earth like?"

Jake tilted his head and said ruefully. "That's rather like asking a Risonian to describe our planet, but one who is Tizzalurian and has never seen your capital city, Marasca. Or

41

the Holla Sea. Because Earth is a huge planet and there's so much variety."

"Put that way," Utz said, "it makes sense. Where were you on Earth?"

"Three places." Another Bo-See stepped in to pluck a glass from Jake's tray. "A beach at Gulf Shores, Alabama in the southern United States. The city of Seattle on the Pacific Ocean, still in the U.S. And Edinburgh in the north part of the United Kingdom."

"That's all?" Utz's disappointment was obvious. "What about Tokyo? Or Cape Town? Or Jerusalem?"

Jake shook his head. "Those were all the way around the world from where I was. It would've taken days to travel to any of them. And lots of money." He hesitated. "Utz. Isn't that a family name from way back?"

"Of course, you would know that bit of history," Utz said with amusement. "I'm supposed to be just like my great-grandfather."

The Bo-See Coalition was ruled by a monarchy. Succession wasn't a strict inheritance from father to child; instead, within the ruling clan, they fought for the throne, sometimes brutal violent fights. When the Seehafer and Boadan families cross-married over 100 years ago, one ruler could claim the throne through both families, and he named it the Bo-See Coalition after the two families. That ruler, Utz Seehafer, had a Boada mother, Didi Feeney Boada, and a Seehafer father, Hedley Seehafer. It was whispered that Hedley had won Didi in a game of chance, but she'd slit the throat of any who dared repeat that tale. The original Utz's legacy was to unite the two sides of the throne and bring a reign of peace that lasted over 100 years. That was until five years ago when the threat of planetary extinction brought violence back to the forefront.

In those explosive five years, three rulers had been called out and forced to battle—and had lost their lives. The current ruler was Pharomond Seehafer who was both tall and broad, almost a giant. He terrified everyone and had already fought off two challenges to his rule.

Of course, Jake knew the bit of history about Utz's name. He was a Quad-de.

"We are honored that King Seehafer has come to this council," Jake said formally. "Your presence is also appreciated."

"Do you really think this Earth doctor can find a cure for the illness caused by the *umjaadi*?"

The question didn't surprise Jake. Surely the Seehafers would have spies everywhere and knew what was going on. In the last twenty years, they'd lost the political advantage because they didn't support technology, including spaceships. If not for the Quad-de family pouring their fortunes into spaceships and the Moon Base, Risonians wouldn't even have that limited option for saving a fragment of their world. Most of those on the Cadee Moon Base were Tizzalurian, although Swann had tried to bring the best of other countries—space was just too limited. And prejudices limited others from accepting Tizzalurian help.

"Dr. Mangot is a Phoke doctor, not a human. It's only the Phoke who are affected, but they control the seas, and therefore, we must gain their trust. It's crucial that she gets what she needs," Jake said. And silently, he added, she must cure Em. Sometimes, when he was alone, he pulled out his smart phone from Earth and flipped through pictures of Em, or he watched a video of her winning a swim meet.

Utz took the last piece of cheese and golden *wolkev* from Jake's tray. "You know, they won't go for it. Too much to swallow."

Jake stared at him in dismay. A dozen replies came to mind, but he rebutted each himself. In the face of extinction, the only thing the Bo-See had left was dignity. And the ability to play one last card. Did the Bo-See realize what their refusal would mean?

"And if it was you who decided," Jake said softly, "would you let our doctor in your waters?"

Utz took a step closer and spoke softer. "Let me ask you a question. On Earth, how will the alliances go? Will Phoke and Risonians be united because they are both water creatures? Or will the Phoke and humans be allies?"

"That's the burning question of the hour," Jake said. "No one knows how it will turn out. But of course, Dr. Mangot's research will help determine that."

Utz nodded slowly. Even softer, he asked, "And when Risonians reach Earth, will they scatter across the planet? Or will the Bo-See and Tizzalurians remain united against Earth?"

Jake sucked in a breath. "You're going to Earth?"

Utz gave a curt nod and watched Jake work it out. If the Bo-See's prince went to Earth, he'd be a natural leader of that Risonian faction. And if Jake's mother—and maybe eventually Jake himself—led the Tizzalurians, then they needed to be allies. Risonians needed a united front.

"Does your father know?"

"Not yet. I'll find a time to tell him soon."

"And what do you want from me?"

"A promise that you'll listen, that you'll always remember that we are the same species," Utz said. Passion filled his voice and made Jake step back slightly to think.

It wouldn't be a binding alliance, not without hashing out details. There would be many, many details once they reached Earth. But Utz was right; they were the same species, with the same needs. Somehow, they needed a united front against the humans and Phoke.

"We'll be united," Jake said. "But I think we need the Phoke, and Dr. Mangot is one of their senior leaders. What if, despite what the council decides, we go to the southern seas?"

"That would not be wise," came the flat answer.

Utz's body language shifted, and he seemed to tower over Jake. Utz wasn't taller, but certainly broader, and his arms came far down his leg and would have a long reach. Jake didn't want to face him in a street fight or on the fight floor.

Jake sighed in exasperation. It was clear that the Bo-See and Tizzalura should remain allies. But Utz wanted allies when he wasn't willing to give something in return. I'm not good at politics, Jake thought with disgust

"Excuse me," Jake said abruptly. "I must fill up my tray and play the host."

"Of course." Utz waved a path toward the kitchen.

Jake was glad to escape and decided that he didn't want to ever spar with Utz, not even verbal sparring. But clearly, everything had changed in their relationship, and they were reluctant allies. Now they just needed to figure out how not to kill each other.

That night, after the party for officials, Jake returned to find the Earth team gathered in Swann's study room, the one with steps down into the water. Dr. Mangot walked along the bookshelves studying them and occasionally touching one or another. Captain Bulmer and Blake were seated in chairs that automatically adjusted to their body-shape. The chairs were so comfortable that a person was tempted to try to read everything in Swann's library at one seating. Books had evolved since the Risonians had met Earth, with its historical passion for print books. Earthlings had had access to digital books for forty years, but still the print books still ruled.

Rison, of course, had gone to electronic books and documents long ago, except for ceremonial things like birth and marriage documents. But after Rison met Earth, there had been a slow retro-print movement. The Quad-de estate was old enough to have seen print books, moved to electronic books and was now back to print. The library held storage banks of electronic data, along with old and antique versions of digital readers to be able to access even the oldest of digital documents. However, it also had shelves for print books. Swann's father had even collected some print books—through smugglers—from Earth.

"We must talk about what to do next," Jake said.

Dr. Mangot sat in a chair right beside the water, and her bare feet splashed playfully. "I'm worried about Risonians coming to Earth. We don't know how their body's chemistry will affect Earth's environment."

Blake leaned forward, his elbows on his knees. "If we allow Risonians to evacuate to Earth, it's the lesson of the book and movie, *Jurrasic Park*: life will escape! You may try to quarantine everyone who's ever swum in the Risonian seas, but you can't do it. Cross-contamination will eventually happen. It will force an eco-system upheaval that combines Earth and Risonian systems into something new and different. Earth—as we know it—will die. But it's already happening because of Seastead. Our fate is now tied to that of Rison."

Captain Bulmer said, "You're right. However, on Earth, ecologically, I don't think we're at the point of no return. No one knows. But it's certain that if thousands of Risonians evacuate to Earth, it will soon reach that point."

"But I swam in the oceans," Jake said. "And Mom swam in the oceans."

"Hmm," Dr. Mangot turned to look at him. "That means you are both living petri dishes of organisms that live on Earth and on Rison."

Jake waded into the water and went down a step. Bending to splash his knees, he said, "I get what you're saying. Once we swam in Earth's oceans, we were contaminated by the water in which we swam. Mom is an example of a Risonian who has swum in both." Straightening, he shook his head, "But what we really need is a Phoke who has swum in both."

Dr. Mangot stared at him. "Say that again."

"What? That we need a Phoke who has swum in both?"

"Yes. As soon as I swim here on Rison, I'll have to be quarantined, too." The color drained out of her face. She pulled her legs up out of the water and hugged her knees to her chest. "I'll be contaminated. But I can't find the *umjaadi* and understand it without swimming."

"Wait," Blake said. "You mean that if you swim here, you won't swim again on Earth for—well, till you find a cure, even if it takes years?"

Captain Bulmer stepped forward and put a hand on Dr. Mangot's shoulder. "Bea, you don't have to do it. I can."

She looked up at him with gratitude. "I know you'd spare me. But I have to do this."

"It'll kill you to never go back to Aberforth Hills."

"It's not forever. It's just for a time, while we do the research."

Captain Bulmer bent to consider her face. "Bea, it might be forever. You must weigh the odds. Are you willing to take the risk of never seeing Aberforth Hills again?"

Dr. Mangot spun toward Swann's empty desk and then turned back to the water in front of her, as if looking for a way out. "What if I wore eye goggles and kept my mouth shut?"

She looked from one to another, but each person turned away.

"Aberforth Hills," she moaned softly to herself. "I've always put you first."

"Bea, you don't have to do this. Let me do it," Captain Bulmer repeated softly.

"Don't you see? I've never had my own life; it's always been at the beck and call of Aberforth Hills. She has my loyalty and always will. But if I do this, if I dive into this water—" she waved at the waves lapping at the steps and shook her head. "I may never see her again." She was bent over in despair.

Blake stepped forward, took Dr. Mangot's hands and pulled her upright. They stared at each other, tears running down Dr. Mangot's cheeks.

Blake said, "These are desperate times for many of us. And I suspect we'll do even more desperate things than this before it's all over. Yours isn't the first or the last of the tragic lives that will result from the destruction of Rison."

Dr. Mangot stood even taller, her determination growing before their eyes. "Come," she said harshly, "Let's go swimming."

The room was silent, and then Blake nodded, followed by Captain Bulmer. It was decided.

Jake waved toward the far corner and said, "There are spare bathing suits in the changing rooms. Blake, will you swim, too? Do you need to get your scuba gear?"

About ten minutes later, everyone was lined up on the steps.

Dr. Mangot wore a black one-piece suit, showing her age with her stocky figure. Blake wore swimming trunks, along with his scuba tank, mask and breathing regulator. Captain Bulmer wore swimming trunks like Blake's.

Jake handed out slates and writing tools so they could communicate underwater. "I'll take us on a tour of the house and then out for a quick swim in the deeper water. Thirty minutes and we'll be back."

Everyone nodded.

Jake motioned for them to enter the water, but no one took a step.

With a sigh, Jake went down a couple steps and looked back at Blake. He held out his hand and when Blake took it, Jake jerked him hard, making him his fall forward. Blake roared up out of the water and leapt for Jake, submerging them both. They came up laughing.

"Come on in!" Jake cried.

Captain Bulmer and Dr. Mangot held hands and walked stoically down the steps. Dad stood up to adjust his face mask and breathing regulator, and then submerged again.

It was done. Each person—human, Phoke, and half-Risonian-half-human—was a petri dish, a living laboratory of how Rison would interact with each species.

ONE WORLD, ONE GALAXY

January 15
United Nations, New York City, northern hemisphere of Earth
On a calm, cold winter day, Colonel Lett and Colonel Barbena snapped to attention as Ambassador Dayexi Quad-de stepped out of her limousine. Wearing dress whites, the Risonian officers were far more than just ceremonial. They scanned the crowd for suspicious activity, and through earpieces, they constantly talked with United Nations' security. Earth had a long history of dealing with difficult people by assassinating them. The Ambassador's body guards took it seriously.

"Barbarian," Dayexi had told Colonel Lett. If an argument arose on Rison, the feuding parties would meet on the fight floor. Decisions would be finalized in a fair knife fight. What Earth called guerrilla warfare was unthinkable on Rison. It would be considered ultimate cowardice to assassinate a leader.

Head high, very aware of the video cameras, the Ambassador Dayexi Quad-de—known across Earth as the Face of Rison—strode into the United Nations building, followed by her bodyguards. She wore a red pants suit that emphasized her slim figure and curly hair, and lent her an air of authority.

Built in 2030, the new UN building was made of bulletproof glass and reinforced steel that would resist anything short of a nuclear bomb. Its many layers of security made it as safe a place as possible for politicians from around the world.

Everyone in the Assembly Room stood when she entered. The room was packed with shrewd representatives from virtually all the countries on Earth. From conservative black suits to colorful ethnic costumes, the diversity was astounding.

I should be encouraged by the diversity, Dayexi thought. Instead, it made her think of the political struggles on Rison when such a group gathered. She'd have to be wary today. This would be a tough crowd to convince of anything.

She paused, uncertain where to go, but an assistant was there to point the way to an aisle that led down to the front. The room shimmered with colored light from the stained-glass maps.

Maps. Of the world. Of the oceans. Of the solar system. Of the Milky Way. Reproductions of ancient maps. Slick contemporary global maps.

Dayexi had loved this room from the first time she came to speak on behalf of Rison. The maps spoke of how the different countries and societies were connected. That's what she had to emphasize today.

She climbed the steps to the podium and shook the Secretary General's hand.

Dayexi waved at the motto on the wall behind her. "One world. One galaxy." She said, "That gives me hope."

"Hmmm," replied the Secretary General.

Dayexi understood. The building's architect had etched the words in stone without asking permission. To remove it, they'd either have to grind down the stone or replace the stone. Neither was happening soon. She knew that most people hated the words. Still, they were there, and her speech would be given underneath that motto. She'd never met the architect, but she said blessings on his name.

Looking out at the assembly, there were men and women of literally every size, shape and color. Career diplomats, they were among the most cynical of people. And this was it. News from Rison was grim; only days left before the planet died. The United Nations Assembly must give permission today to evacuate her people.

Dayexi shivered. If she failed today, then she had failed her people.

THE RISONIAN
INTERNATIONAL COUNCIL

At the stroke of ten, the appointed time, Swann Quad-de, Prime Minister of Tizzalura, rose from his place at the conference tables. They were arranged in a square to avoid the appearance that anyone actually led the council. Translators were stationed carefully so they could translate back and forth from Tizzalurian, Boadan, and other minor languages.

Some members were still absent, but Prime Minister Quad-de always started on time. He began, "Esteemed leaders—"

The musicians positioned in the room's corner struck up the Risonian world song, a recent addition to the Council's ceremony. No one knew the song, a mishmash of cultures and mangled words. Last year, Jake's mother had insisted he learn the words, but he detested it. Still, he joined the throng and obediently stood while the music swirled.

In the midst of it, His Majesty Pharomond Seehafer entered, along with his retinue. Colorful, flashy, barbaric—the Bo-See always went for a grand entrance. King Seehafer strode confidently toward the table, singing at full volume.

Jake winced. He recognized now that the song sounded like a Bo-See ballad, a musical form that he didn't like. It explained why Seehafer could sing it so lustily.

Just as the song ended, Seehafer arrived at his chair, which was opposite Swann's. Seehafer wore a sparkling diadem, and strapped to his waist was a huge golden *thron*, a hefty battle-axe. Some said it had been handed down to Bo-See leaders for a hundred years. Others believed it was wielded by the original Utz Seehafer himself. The king's bodyguards drew out the heavy chair, and Seehafer sat. Tall, he was a head above everyone else except Swann. Clearly, this was a ruler to be respected.

Swann crossed his arms, frowned, and nodded to Seehafer.

King Seehafer crossed his arms, nodded back to Swann, and sat back with a wide grin. "Shall we begin? Meetings should always begin on time."

Swann motioned for the rest of the assembly to sit. His tight mouth told Jake that he was aggravated. Somehow, he managed to keep his voice calm and steady. "Esteemed leaders from around our world, we are here to consider weighty matters."

Jake, from his place behind Swann's chair, tuned out the politician's rhetoric. He felt a guilty pang, knowing that his best friend on earth, David Gordon, would have hung on every word. Each delegate had the right to make opening statements, so it would be an hour before the Earth delegation was even introduced. He'd have to quietly translate then, so he didn't feel too bad about tuning out now.

Jake spent the time studying the Bo-See delegates. Utz Seehafer, the heir apparent, stood behind his father's chair as an observer, just as Jake stood behind Swann. When Utz met his eye, Jake nodded coolly. Utz gave the tiniest nod back. To Seehafer's right was a man, dressed in scarlet, who Jake didn't know. Jake leaned toward Norio, who stood beside him, and whispered, "Who is that?"

From the side of his mouth, Norio said, "Ancel Fallstar, the smuggler."

Jake's eyes went wide. Seehafer was openly bringing a smuggler to the negotiations. That didn't bode well for the outcome. Three young women, also wearing scarlet, stood behind Fallstar.

Norio leaned in and added, "And his daughters. They captain his spaceships."

Not surprising, Jake thought. Fallstar would make sure his daughters escaped Rison. What better way than to give them each a starship? That probably meant—Jake glared at the Fallstar daughters—that one of them had shot across the bow of the *Eagle 10* and made them pay a toll to come down to Rison. He'd probably never find out which one, and that rankled.

To Seehafer's left, General Yancy Pender sat stiffly upright, refusing to relax or let his back touch his chair. His braided beard declared him as a Bo-See military leader. Jake had heard that he was a staunch supporter of King Seehafer. Military might was almost meaningless now, though, with the impending destruction of Rison. An interesting choice of retinue.

"Any scientists?" he whispered to Norio.

Norio shook his head and whispered back, "All military."

Jake pondered the meaning of the military dominance in the Bo-See Coalition's delegates. They were clearly ready for war. Were the Bo-See ripe for yet another coup? Jake's gaze went back to Pharomond and his muscled arms. You'd have to be a fool to ever challenge him on the fight floor.

After standing so long, Jake shifted uneasily trying to ease the ache beginning in his calves. A glare from Norio, though, made Jake stiffen and stop fidgeting. Swann was speaking again, and Jake tried to pay attention.

"We thank you for your opening statements. I'd like to introduce Earth's Medical Mission team, who will be making a short presentation."

Jake turned toward the door and watched the team file in. Blake wore his dress whites, which showed off his lean physique. Very formal and correct, Captain Bulmer wore his royal blue uniform of the Aberforth Hills Militia. Dr. Mangot wore a royal blue dress that skimmed the floor, skirts swirling gracefully. With each step, Jake's tension increased. This was an important moment for Earth, for Rison, and for Em. They must get approval from the International Council, or their mission would take far longer than anyone wanted.

As agreed, Jake left his position beside his father and joined the group so he could translate. They hoped Jake's family ties would lend more credibility to Earth's Medical Mission.

It was time for Jake's rehearsed speech. "Lords and Ladies of Rison, I return from off-planet to my beloved Rison."

A round of unexpected applause forced Jake to stop. He was surprised that anyone cared that he'd been off-planet. His parents had more good will than they knew because it wasn't from anything he did or was.

When the applause subsided, he continued. "I bring with me a team of scientists from Earth. Rison's own Seastead team accidentally released an *umjaadi* organism, which has infected the Phoke, Earth's aquatic people. From the Phoke people, meet Dr. Beatrice Mangot and Captain Heath Bulmer." Jake stopped to bow to them. He was amused with himself for falling so easily into the formality of such a conference.

Captain Bulmer responded with a bow while Dr. Mangot curtsied. When she rose Dr. Mangot took a half-step forward.

Afraid she would start talking too soon, Jake continued, "Sadly, if our peoples are to have a future, it will be as pilgrims on Earth, our sister blue planet. We must have their cooperation, and in turn, we must work to find ways to give them the cooperation they need." Never had Jake felt so uncertain. The finely turned political phrase was always three times longer than plain communication called for. He noticed that no one was cheering for him now.

King Seehafer put his hands on his chair to stand, but Ancel Fallstar rose first. Jake saw Swann grimace slightly, but he didn't understand why.

Fallstar spoke loud and forceful, saying, "You say that our future lies on Earth. And yet you bring us no word that Earth will accept our people. Still, Ambassador Quad-de waits and waits and waits. Pah! We'll beg no more. The Bo-See choose to face our fate and live fully right up until our last moments. So, why should we cooperate with these Phoke from Earth?"

Scorn etched his face and words. Behind him, his expression was mirrored by his daughters. Jake translated easily, trying to stay only a phrase behind.

A roar arose from around the conference table. It was easy to see that Earth's delays had created bitter resentment. Each day of delay meant fewer people would escape Rison's destruction. Each day meant a loved one—a wife, daughter, son, aunt, uncle, mother, father, grandmother, or grandfather—would die.

If Earth had only accepted Rison's plea for help a year ago! But, Jake thought, that would mean even greater crowding on Earth. The politics on Earth were just as bad as here on Rison. Crowds of refugees were never welcome.

Swann rose now and called for quiet so he could speak. "It is true that Earth has been slow in making a decision. But now, with time so crucial, we need to think about the survival of our species. What does it matter if the Earth medical team swims in our seas? What does it matter if they infect our seas? Who will live long enough for it to matter? But for the Phoke, it can matter, and matter a great deal."

"And we care about the Phoke because. . .?" Fallstar responded with a flourish of his hands. His robes were startlingly scarlet against the Phoke's blue and the U.S. Navy's white uniforms.

Again, Jake noticed that Swann winced at Fallstar's words. Jake closed his eyes to gather his thoughts.

Dr. Mangot could be silent no longer and answered, "You care about us because we are sentient creatures such as your-selves."

Jake struggled to keep up the translation into Risonian, so her passion would be understood.

"You cannot turn a hard heart to us in our hour of need. Because you want to die with dignity, the dignity that comes from knowing you've done the right thing, even when no one else has done right. This isn't about Earth turning their backs on you. It's about who you are, as a people, as a planet. You're better than Earth." She took a big breath, stepped forward and held out her hands in appeal. "We know that you could have attacked us but you've take the high moral ground. You came in peace. You appealed to our better side, and I hope that in the end, Earth will come through. But even if she doesn't. . ." Dr. Mangot's voice was choked with emotion. "Even if she doesn't, you must still walk the narrow path, you must still choose to do the right thing."

King Seehafer spoke with a deep, booming voice. "Easy for you to say. Your people will live. Mine will die."

Dr. Mangot nodded. "Except mine will die, too, unless Ri-son helps us."

They stared at each other for long moments. Then, King Seehafer deliberately turned away from the Phoke. He straightened and faced Swann. His face was hard and his voice harsh, "Prime Minister Quad-de, we asked you a question and you have yet to answer it. Why should we care about Earth's Phoke race when Earth cares nothing for us?"

ॐ ॐ

Jake wanted to put his face in his hands and weep. Why were the Bo-See always so hard to deal with? If only Pharomond Seehafer wasn't their leader. For a moment, he allowed himself to believe that the leadership was all that mattered. What if Pharomond Seehafer wasn't the leader?

A sudden, wild idea came to Jake. The only way to unseat a Bo-See King was to challenge his leadership on the fight floor. Jake could do that.

I'd die.

But if he didn't do it, all the Phoke would die, including Em. He had vowed to do anything to save her, even if it meant he didn't come home. Anything. Did he really mean it?

I'm not good enough on the fight floor.

His heart beat faster; he automatically wiggled his foot to feel the knife strapped on his right leg and shrugged his shoulders to feel the knife at the base of his back. It felt good to have the knives back in place; he'd missed them on Earth.

Maybe he wasn't good enough to win. But if he tried, if he challenged the King to fight, King Seehafer would have to respond. But it was a move too desperate to even think of—yet.

Another idea came to him, and he said, "Prime Minister, the Earth mission team asks that each delegate cast his or her own vote, and that the votes are secret ballots." Maybe they could find a chink in the unanimous front of the Bo-See.

King Seehafer smirked and leaned back in his chair. He said nothing, letting his retinue speak instead.

"We respectfully decline to vote as individuals," Ancel Fallstar said. "We will vote as a block because we are united in purpose."

Jake looked across the faces of those on the Bo-See side of the table. "Does no one challenge the King's vote?"

Immediately, everyone turned their backs on Jake. Of course, it was an insult to suggest any Bo-See vote against his king. But these were desperate times. Still, no one broke rank; no one even looked indecisive.

Jake realized that the King of the Bo-See did hold a cast-iron position. Pharomond must be removed. He must be taken out, but there's only one way to do that: the fight floor.

Do I dare take that chance? Of course not.

The discussion raged all morning with each side repeating its position and giving no concessions or compromises. By lunch time, everyone was mentally exhausted. Jake found he couldn't even eat the sticky buns brought from his favorite

Tizzalurian bakery. Despair dogged his steps as he carried trays of refreshments for the delegates.

And yet the Bo-See still hadn't said, "No." They were still listening, and surely something would break through the impasse, and they would agree to let the team go south.

After lunch, the discussions continued with no progress till about mid-afternoon when an official slipped in and handed a note to Swann. After glancing at it, he rose with a smile.

"Esteemed leaders," he said. "I believe we have some progress to report. Ambassador Dayexi Quad-de wants to speak directly to you. We are setting up a large screen in the adjacent room. If you'll kindly follow me, we'll hear her report."

EARTH'S DECISION

"Greetings from Earth!" said Ambassador Quad-de.

The large screen was surprisingly clear considering that the signal was traveling across light years to reach them. There would be a time-delay of several seconds, of course, so questions and answers were hard. But receiving an ansible announcement was an amazing technology. The translators positioned themselves near those who needed it.

Mom's dark hair flopped in limp curls, and she had dark circles under her eyes. She looked exhausted, but her voice was excited. "Esteemed leaders, I've just come from talking to the Assembly at Earth's United Nations. They voted and the answer is YES! We may start evacuation immediately. Send the ships! Tell them to launch today! Tonight! Within the hour!"

The room erupted in laughter and shouts of joy.

Jake hugged Blake and they cried together, "Saved!"

But the Ambassador was still speaking, not knowing that few were still listening. Jake shushed people around him.

". . .not the best situation. Our people will not be allowed to swim in Earth's oceans until the *umjaadi* organism is contained. Until then, Earth will provide housing in China, in the Gobi Desert in the Altai Mountains. China has an installation there that will be suitable. They will immediately build swimming pools for us, so that by the time the first ships arrive, they will be ready. It's a triumph for us today! We have a safe place for our people. Send the ships!"

Jake's heart dropped. Earth agreed for Risonians to come, but they planned to quarantine them in a desert? No water. If it was bad on the Cadee Moon Base, with people aching for a swim, what would it be like in a desert? They'd be cooped up in shoddy housing for years! Jake had seen videos of refugee camps across the Earth. This was all wrong. It might look like a success on the surface, and maybe it was the best Mom could do, but it was terrible.

Apparently, King Seehafer agreed. "What nonsense is this? Quarantine us in a desert? Are they mad?"

Dr. Mangot stepped in. "Of course, they're mad." She motioned to Jake to translate, and he repeated her words. "You've forced us to accept your people, but that doesn't mean we have to threaten our seas. But know this: the Phoke have powerful people in positions worldwide. We can change the tide of opinion. If we wish." Her face turned just as hard as King Seehafer's. "I need access to the southern seas to save my people. If you allow that, we'll turn our influence toward finding your people a more suitable place to live."

Before Seehafer could speak, a scarlet slash of color stomped up to Dr. Mangot.

Ancel Fallstar roared, "No. This half-hearted invitation to share the planet of Earth—it's an insult. No. You'll never be allowed to search our seas for a cure to the *umjaadi*. Never."

There. He had said it. Never.

Other southerners nodded agreement. They spoke with one voice.

King Seehafer shrugged, "There. We have spoken. Finally."

THE CHALLENGE

Jake's heart beat a tattoo on his chest.

Really, Em, I have no other choice.

Jake marched up to King Seehafer. "My Lord," he called loudly, and paused until he had the attention of everyone in the room. "My Lord," he repeated. Words almost failed him, but he thought of Em the last day he'd seen her, walking on the shore of the North Sea, pale and trusting. He thought of his words, "I swear to you, I'll bring back a cure for the *umjaadi*."

If possible, he stood even straighter. "My Lord, I challenge you to the fight floor. I will fight you to become the ruler of the Bo-See Coalition."

King Seehafer shook his head as if he hadn't heard right. "Challenge? Me?"

"Yes," nodded Jake. "You aren't leading your people toward a brighter future. You're unfit to be leader." He gulped as he heard himself speaking insults, but he couldn't stop. "The Bo-See Coalition needs a leader who will boldly lead them off-planet. I can do that."

Across the room, Jake saw Swann, his face a mask of unbelief and anguish.

King Seehafer stepped closer to Jake and bent his head to Jake's level. The King's eyes glittered like a black diamond forged in a volcano. "You want to challenge me?"

Jake nodded glumly.

King Seehafer threw back his head and guffawed. He slapped Jake's back, almost knocking him down. The king threw out his hands to the crowd. "Did you hear? He wants to challenge me!"

Now, the crowd joined in the joke, laughing with incredulity at Jake's foolishness.

Even Utz shook his head and laughed.

King Seehafer grabbed Jake's arm and tugged, hauling him over to Swann. "Did you hear your son's amusing challenge?"

Swann started, "Sir, he's young—"

"Yes," interrupted King Seehafer. "Young. And yet, he's braver than the lot of you." Now, the king pulled Jake to him in a dramatic hug. "Bravely done," he murmured.

Ancel Fallstar called, "You won't fight him?"

"Of course not," said King Seehafer. "He's young and foolish. Why should he end his life now?"

No one is taking me seriously! Jake shoved away from Seehafer and said fiercely, "I will fight you."

He dropped a knife from his arm holster and brandished it.

Seehafer guffawed. "Put it up, son. You've earned my respect today by your boldness and bravery. But don't ruin it by forcing me to kill you."

Swann put a hand on Jake's arm. "Jake. Put it up."

Jake realized that he'd overstepped, that he'd never be able to defeat the Bo-See Coalition's king. He was lucky to be alive right now. He straightened and bowed to the King and his courtiers who had drawn nearer to protect the king if needed. "My Lord." His voice stuck. "Please. Allow the Earthlings access to your seas."

The room was utterly still, waiting for the King to respond.

King Seehafer waved a hand at the ansible screen. "After the Ambassador's announcement, we have much to discuss. I will give you an answer tomorrow."

A wave of relief passed through Jake, and his knees almost buckled. He was alive. He had demanded an answer from the most dangerous man on Rison and was still alive. He inclined his head in answer, "My Lord. We thank you."

As soon as the king turned away, Jake almost collapsed. But Swann was there to hold him up.

"That was the craziest and most courageous thing I've ever seen!" Even Swann was looking at Jake with new eyes.

But Jake just sank into a chair, closed his eyes and put his head down between his legs to keep from fainting.

THE BO-SEE

The fight floor was brightly lit when King Pharomond Seehafer and Ancel Fallstar entered to spar in a practice fight. No knives, just wrestling.

Utz watched King Seehafer stomp a bare foot on the dirt, testing how well it was packed. He wore tight fight pants but was bare-chested, revealing massive chest muscles. Fallstar wore the same wrestling uniform, except his pants were scarlet instead of black. Scars scattered around both men's torsos and arms. They circled, each waiting for the other to make the first move.

It was a private fight floor on the grounds of the Quad-de estate, housed in a small round building. The floor was traditional bare dirt, and Ancel could cross it in ten easy paces. Smooth metal walls rose twice as tall as Pharomond. Above were tiers of viewing stands, virtually empty. Each man had two bodyguards, and each had brought his children as witnesses.

Utz had gotten a key to the building from Jake and would lock it back when they finished. He watched the Fallstar daughters with caution. Fallstar had always wanted boys, but was given instead five daughters. Two were young enough that they were home with their mother. The older three who attended the council with their father were lithe and strong. Utz didn't think he'd want to meet them on the fight floor. They refused his offer of refreshments and sat watching their father with impassive faces.

Utz turned to the fight floor. Up close, Fallstar looked old. His blond beard was sprinkled with white hairs, and his skin was wrinkled from a lifetime in the sun and wind. His nose ridges were sharp and deep.

"What do you think of the Ambassador's announcement?" Seehafer said.

Fallstar shrugged. "You know that neither of us is going to Earth." He lunged, diving for Seehafer's legs, but Seehafer danced away quickly, leaving Ancel to slide across the dirt floor. The women cheered while Fallstar rose and dusted off his pants.

"Of course," said Seehafer. "But what of your daughters?" He attacked suddenly, a flurry of kicks aimed at Fallstar's head.

Fallstar casually blocked the kicks with his arms. He glanced up at the scarlet-robed women. "They are Risonians to the end." He lifted his chin toward Utz. "And I assume the same for your son."

"Good. We agree." Seehafer stepped in, grabbed Fallstar's arms and heaved him over his head to fall flat on the ground.

Utz nodded at his father's efficiency. But he wondered if he'd missed something important. Were they talking about not getting himself and the Seehafer daughters off-planet; saying that they wouldn't even attempt it? He stiffened. He desperately wanted to take Derry and go to Earth, but that would mean leaving his father behind. Unthinkable.

Or were Seehafer and Fallstar in agreement that they should evacuate their sons and daughters? Suspicious, Utz watched Fallstar carefully, making sure to keep his daughters in view, also.

Fallstar slowly rose and shook his head to clear it. He held up a hand, asking for time to recover.

Utz grinned at the Fallstar daughters to remind them that King Seehafer had won his position fairly on the fight floor and would defend it there any time. He hoped they recognized his gloating.

Seehafer graciously stepped back to give Fallstar a moment. "And these aliens, should we let them swim in our waters?"

"No," Fallstar said shortly. "Never." He stepped back into the fight and grappled Seehafer. Both bent over, heads butting and arms reaching out to find an advantage, a momentary weakness, a slight imbalance.

With their heads down, Seehafer grunted and said, "Some might say you are foolish to say no to the Earthlings."

Fallstar shoved hard and raised up to stand, glaring at Seehafer.

Seehafer held up his hands and chided softly, like he was talking to a child. "Ancel! You can't kill all those Phoke on Earth."

"Why not?" Fallstar's voice was harsh and loud. "They have killed millions of our people by delaying their decision. We should have attacked—" He stopped himself with visible effort, swallowing hard and turning his face aside.

That decision, Utz thought, was far in the past and there was no reason to bring it up except it would always be a gall to the Bo-See Coalition. They would never forgive the Quaddes for refusing them spaceships to attack. Five years ago, three years ago, they could've won. Easily. Utz thought of the old Navy Captain on the Earth team and his mouth curled in a sneer. But it faded fast. It was too late now for an invasion.

Fallstar continued, "Earth will finally allow us to come, but only if we agree to live in a desert. Bah!" He waved a hand to dismiss the idea. Sidling along the metal wall, he tried to get behind Seehafer.

But Seehafer turned so that he kept facing Fallstar. He shook his head. "They are harsh. We understand that they are trying to protect their planet—and by extension that means all of us who will take refuge there. We—" he hesitated, and then continued with an ironic note, "—appreciate that. But it's too little, too late."

Fallstar smiled wickedly. "Then we agree?"

Seehafer smiled back. "Agreed."

The men straightened and bowed to each other, the sparring done for the day.

Seehafer slapped Fallstar's back and they turned to the door in the wall.

"One other thing," Fallstar said. "What will be do about the young Quad-de who wants to fight you?"

"I have an idea about that," Seehafer said. The door closed behind them shutting out the conversation.

Utz let himself relax slightly. This had gone well. The Bo-See would vote with a united front, as tradition demanded. Somehow, though, he felt like he'd missed something. There were deeper issues than he understood. It was like Fallstar and his father understood each other without speaking.

Utz found himself wishing that he could discuss the day with Derry. Where was she this time of day? Still in the lab? She would immediately identify the tiny thing that was bothering him.

He mentally reviewed the discussion again but saw noth-ing unusual. So why did it leave him with a deep unease?

THE VOTE

The Earth team chose to swim Risonian waters again, and had swum far into the night, only returning about midnight. Famished after the exercise, they ate and talked about the Risonian sea life and only found their beds in the early morning hours. Jake had slept two hours and woken unsettled.

He spent a half hour talking with Swann, who also couldn't sleep, and finally, gone for a walk. He slipped out the front doors of the Quad-de estate. He wanted to wander the streets of Killia, the city of his childhood. He loved this city and wanted to wander its streets one last time.

Walking across the courtyard, ash kicked up at his heels. Soon, the servants would arrive to sweep it clean again, such a futile effort.

He strolled the main boulevard of Killia for a few minutes, seeing ghosts of his past: his barber, his favorite pastry shop, his doctor's office. Finally, he turned onto a familiar street leading toward the city's park. There, he climbed a grassy hillock that gave him a vista of the city. Despite the smog, the city skyline was familiar. The newly risen sun was at his back, bathing everything in a golden glow: the dome of city government, the delicate spire of the art museum, the bulky stadium that housed a popular fight floor, and the banking buildings that his ancestors had built.

From here, the volcanoes loomed dark on the horizon, lazily spewing out white steam. He turned away, trying to ignore them.

The streets were deserted this early. An ash-covered *kriga*, a monkey-like creature, scampered across the grass and leapt into a tree; it was scrawny, probably the pet of someone who had died, and it had gone feral. It reminded him of his pet *kriga*, Bell, whom he hadn't thought of in months. Leaving Bell behind had been wrenching. That was so long ago, when he was just a child.

A noise, just at the edge of his awareness, suddenly caught his attention and held it: the songs of the volcanoes. Musical and deep, like a bass soloist. Underneath Killia's traffic noise and the morning vendors just opening shops, magma burbled, chugged and whooshed. The song was almost lulling, a constant noise that told Jake to relax because he was home. The planet was singing under his feet, singing the song of a water planet with a molten core.

He stopped short.

No, it wasn't comforting. It was the sound of a time bomb gurgling away the moments until the end.

He turned back to the Quad-de estate, alternately stomping and running. Those stubborn Bo-See! The Phoke needed that cure, and the Risonians needed a new home. Today, they had to fight smarter and harder. Em needed a cure. He vowed to himself again, "I'll do anything."

Only much later did he remember the beauty of Killia and weep for its loss.

Swann Quad-de, Prime Minister of Tizzalura, rose to speak. "Esteemed leaders, welcome to the second day of our council concerning the Earthlings request to do emergency medical research in our southern seas."

The murmuring stopped, and all eyes turned to the Prime Minister.

Jake suppressed a yawn from the late night.

"To shorten the process," Swann said, "I call for an immediate vote on the matter." His authoritative voice carried across the room. One by one, delegates nodded approval.

Surprisingly, Jake heard no objections. That either meant all was well, or all was lost. Blake, again wearing his dress whites, tugged Jake's shirt and pointed to his ear with an annoyed look. Jake had forgotten about being a translator and quickly caught up.

The council's secretary read out the names of the delegates:

"Lord Jochen Bates of the Adler Nation in the far north."

"Aye."

"Lady Ettore Edwards of the Christie Islands of the north."

"Aye."

The northern countries were allies of Tizzalura, so this wasn't a surprise. Neither were the next three votes from the Bo-See Coalition.

"King Pharomond Seehafer, King of the Bo-See Coalition."

"Nay."

"General Yancy Pender, General of the Bo-See Coalition."

"Nay."

"Lord Ancel Fallstar of the Bo-See Coalition."

"Nay."

The battle would be won or lost when the Bo-See's neighbors in the south voted.

The secretary called, "Lord Albion Kulig of the Chadja tribes of the south."

The Chadja delegates sat next to General Pender. The General leaned over and patted Lord Kulig's arm.

Lord Kulig nodded to the General and called, "Nay."

And so, it went. The southern delegates voting no, and the northern delegates voting yes. With each negative vote, Jake's stomach cramped harder. The Bo-See and its neighbors were going to vote down the expedition.

Suddenly, the secretary paused reading names. He swayed, frantically clutching at the table.

A quake!

The planet was shaking harder than Jake had ever felt. Was this it? Would the planet implode, killing them all, and making all of this a moot question?

Jake counted seconds: one, two, three, four, five, six. . .

The shaking stopped.

Jake looked around. Was anyone hurt? One of the Fallstar daughters had fallen and her sisters were pulling her up. General Pender lay sprawled halfway to the doorway, probably an instinctive reaction to run. King Seehafer gripped the arms of his chair, and his eyes were wide.

"Doomsday," said someone.

And then, looking around, everyone was fine. A nervous twitter broke out and spread.

The room shook again, though, harder this time, knocking things off the wall. The floor tilted one way and then another.

Only five seconds.

But this time, people weren't so surprised. They either sat still in their chairs or sat on the floor if needed for balance. Stoic. No one cried out and no one ran.

Jake found that he was hugging the back of his step-father's chair. As the quake quieted, he gulped, tried to straighten, and then hesitantly, he turned loose. The floors were intact and not buckled, but a couple framed portraits of Quad-de ancestors had dropped to the ground, frames shattered.

Ancel Fallstar rose and pointed a hand at Dr. Mangot. "Go home, Phoke, before you die here. You'll never sail the seas of my world. Never. You're alien. Go home. Leave us to die in peace."

With a nod to his daughters to follow, the scarlet-clad family strode out of the room.

Silence reigned.

Despair gripped Jake. Fallstar was an expert Navy man, even if he didn't call his troops a Navy. Smugglers or Navy, it made no difference because they were still the troops that would prevent Dr. Mangot from finding the cure for Em.

He remembered the last time he'd seen Em, walking on Coldingham Beach in the frigid Scottish air. He had put the amber mermaid necklace around her neck and then kissed her, a moment that split his world into before and after. This, right now on Rison, was after the kiss. And he was committed to bringing that cure to Em or die trying.

Grimly, he thought, I may die trying. Somehow, they had to get to the southern seas. Quickly.

Teeth clenched, Jake strode to King Seehafer and stood with his legs spread wide, and his fists on his hips. He demanded, "I will fight you for leadership of the Bo-See Coalition."

King Seehafer was still seated, and at Jake's words, looked amused. "I won't fight a youth such as yourself. Let me put it in Earth terms, since you've lived there so long: It would be like slaughtering a sacrificial lamb."

Jake's stomach twisted in shame and anger. He could do nothing for Em.

"However, to show our respect for your offer, we will allow you to enter the fight floor against my son, Utz Seehafer. We doubt you'll last even five minutes."

"I'll make it five minutes," Jake said with renewed hope. "And when I do, you'll allow us to go south."

Seehafer shook his head, like he was admonishing a very simple-headed child. "No. If you make it five minutes, we'll let you live."

Behind him, Jake heard Swann suck in a breath. But as they had agreed, Swann said nothing and didn't try to interfere.

Jake gulped. "When?"

"Now."

THE FIGHT FLOOR

Back in his room, Utz unrolled his knife bundle and considered which to choose for the fight, as they were allowed to bring three knives onto the fight floor. First, he chose his favorite dagger, used for thrusting or stabbing. For his left hand, Utz preferred a simple T-handled knife, a grip that lent power to a thrust. Likely, he'd only use the dagger, but he wanted blades in both hands just in case there was an opening. He fingered his gut-hook knife made for disemboweling an enemy. But this wouldn't be a fight to the death, so he left it in the bundle. Instead, he picked up his spear-pointed knife, another good knife for thrusting or stabbing. That one he sheathed at his waist for easy access.

King Seehafer walked in alone, his bodyguards waiting outside.

Utz's anger boiled over. "You have me fighting that weakling?"

"Don't underestimate him. He studied with Master Bru Paniego."

Utz stopped short. "I knew he'd studied with someone from Bo-See, but I didn't know it was Master Paniego. Then he'll know something about knife fighting."

King Seehafer nodded. "Before he went off-planet, he was the best Tizzalurian knife fighter I'd ever seen."

"We watched that fight together." Utz nodded. "Then why—"

"Because I want to see what he's really made of. Will he fight well or will he fight as a coward?"

"But why?"

"There are many strings to pull," said Seehafer simply.

Utz understood that. As a child, he'd played the string game often. Groups of Bo-See children entered the fight floor. One child was IT and watched the others. Each child held a long string and a partner took the other end. Then, they wove the strings, dipping over and under, around and through other children until everyone was hopelessly tangled in a nest of string.

IT tried to untangle everyone. Sometimes, IT pulled on a string to see where it ended and what effect it had. IT ordered this child or that to go under, over, through or around to untangle everything. Usually it ended in laughter when IT gave up, but Utz never gave up. He held the record for the longest string game, refusing to allow any of the other children to leave until he had them untangled. Utz had always understood that it was training for politics, that actions and events often originated in places you didn't expect.

But what did that childhood game have to do with the Quad-des?

The audience thronged into the ceremonial fight building and crammed onto the benches. It was larger than the practice building used by Seehafer and Fallstar the day before. But it was still a private fight floor, so it wasn't meant for many spectators. No one wanted to travel far after the quakes that morning, though, so they agreed to stay on the Quad-de estate. As it was, some refused to enter the building for fear of being trapped in a quake.

Seehafer and his retinue sat on the south side while Swann and his retinue sat on the north. The referee was Lord Albion Kulig, the Chadja delegate. He swore to be neutral, but Jake knew that he was aligned with the Bo-See Coalition, so he expected no quarter.

Jake expected no mercy, just as he would give no mercy. He and Utz were well-matched.

Both young men were stripped to their fighting pants. Each carried two knives, one in each hand. Each had a third knife in a sheath at his waist. Jake worried that he hadn't practiced knife fighting enough lately. But he had stayed in shape, and as Master Bru always said, "The fight is won or lost in the mind."

Jake had the motivation needed to win: Em's life.

But Utz was motivated as well: the honor of the Bo-See Coalition.

The referee motioned for both fighters to raise their hands in salute. When the referee dropped his hands, the fight began.

From his days with Master Bru, Jake expected Utz to attack immediately. He watched Utz's hips for a change in direction. When Utz lunged left, Jake shifted right and swiped with his right hand.

A tiny red streak appeared above Utz's navel. First blood!

A roar reverberated in the room, but Jake focused on Utz. Jake saw something change in Utz's face, like he'd been playing around but decided he had to really concentrate.

Good, Jake thought. *I earned his respect within five seconds.*

Before Utz had time to recalculate his strategy, Jake rushed Utz, forcing him against the wall, and then when it came, he danced out of reach of Utz's dagger thrust.

"Rushing seldom scored a cut, but it kept an opponent unsettled," Master Bruniego had said.

Shaking his head, Utz stepped to the center of the floor. Jake kept his distance, and they circled each other. Suddenly, Utz charged. The roar of the crowd ebbed; Jake saw only Utz's dagger. He didn't retreat, but held his ground and parried a jab with his own knife.

The clash of iron-on-iron echoed.

But Jake hadn't watched Utz's left hand, which held a T-shape handled knife. Best for stabbing, Utz jabbed the knife into Jake's leg before Jake shoved him away. Looking down at the pain in his leg, blood spilled from a tear. This wasn't a fight to the death, but Jake realized he needed to finish it soon or he'd lose.

Utz gave him no time to think, charging again. This time, Jake met the charge by grabbing onto Utz's shoulders, falling and throwing him over his head. They both landed on the floor. Stealthily, Jake sheathed his left-handed knife, and dug into the dirt floor. Gripping a handful of dirt in his hands, he rose and turned, waiting for Utz's next charge.

Still wobbly after the fall, Jake was barely ready when Utz barreled toward him. At the last minute, he threw the handful of dirt into Utz's face and spun right, away from Utz's knife. Utz's forward momentum carried him a step past Jake, who brought his fists down onto the back of Utz's shoulders.

Utz fell heavily and Jake leapt onto his back.

Victory! He could feel it. Jake looked up to grin at Swann, when Utz heaved and somehow Jake found his nose ground into the dirt and Utz sitting on his back.

"Yield!" Utz said.

Jake experimentally heaved, but realized that Utz's thick frame was too much for him to move. He dropped his knives and called. "Yield!"

Utz climbed off his back and held out a hand to let Jake up.

"Well fought," Utz said quietly. "You almost had me, if you hadn't stopped to gloat."

Ruefully, Jake smiled. "Thank you. Well fought to you, too."

Inside, he was smiling, too, as relief flooded through him. The fight had gone as he and Swann had expected. They had hoped to use the fight to gain an ally. Only time would tell if they had accomplished their purpose in losing.

૭૦   ૮૭

Walking out of the fight building, Prime Minister Swann Quad-de stopped to speak to King Pharomond Seehafer.

"Congratulations to your son. Utz is a skilled fighter," Swann murmured.

They walked side by side for a moment, their robes a study in contrast, black for Swann versus white for Pharomond.

Pharomond leaned toward Swann and murmured back. "No. You can't come south. The Bo-See stand as a solid front and always will. But I understand the Jewel Islands are lovely this time of year."

Swann nodded companionably. "We thank you for recommending Master Bru for Jake's studies. A noble warrior."

Pharomond smiled, nodded, and walked away.

UNTANGLING THREADS

Jake paced back and forth in front of the stairs leading into the watery depths of the Quad-de's home. The rest of the Earth crew drooped on chairs, emotionally exhausted. They had started the day hopeful. After all, ships streamed out of the Cadee Spaceport all day, and more would follow. Thousands of Risonians were en route for Earth. That should have meant more cooperation from the Risonian Council.

Instead, as the day developed, petty regional politics still ruled.

Dr. Mangot held a bowl of golden *wolkevs* in her lap but hadn't taken a bite of any. "What do we do now?" Her hopes were shattered, her voice empty, as if emotion was forbidden.

Captain Bulmer sat beside her chaise lounge on a chair. He reached over and took a *wolkev* and popped into his mouth. When he was finished chewing, he said. "Lovely fruit. Sort of like a raspberry-banana, except not." When no one answered, he said, "There's always hope. We'll think of something."

"No!" Dr. Mangot said angrily. "Here, eat these." She shoved the bowl at Captain Bulmer and then stood to pace behind Jake. "We've failed. What can we do? We have swum in the ocean, but not in the oceans where there are *umjaadi*. We don't have infections, and we need them!"

"You want to get sick?" Jake raised an eyebrow.

"What if we snuck in anyway?" Captain Bulmer said.

Blake crossed his arms over this chest and growled, "They'd shoot us on the spot."

Jake said hopefully, "We could pretend to go back to the Moon and instead, go south."

"Those Fallstar women would shoot us down," Blake said.

Jake nodded ruefully. "And they wouldn't regret it at all."

Despair made Dr. Mangot look old. "Do we just go back to Earth?" The question was half-whine and half-resignation.

Jake thought about the fight with Utz. He'd won until Utz threw him off. Battles weren't over till they were over. This was politics, the behind-the-scenes events that really ran a nation or world. The council's "No!" meant nothing.

Cheerfully, Jake said, "There's an old saying on Rison: Sometimes, strings untangle in the night."

Dr. Mangot wrinkled her forehead. "What does that mean?"

Blake shrugged. He'd been around Risonians long enough to answer this one. "It's based on an old children's game of untangling threads."

"A children's game!" Dr. Mangot was outraged. "That's all you have to offer right now? A children's game!"

Jake said, "It's either that or politics."

Angrily, Dr. Mangot grabbed the fruit bowl from Captain Bulmer and pitched all the *wolkevs* into the water. She said, "Then, we're lost for sure."

Shaking woke up Jake. Instantly, he popped up, sure that the world was quaking again. He waited, trying to see in his dark room. Rison wasn't moving, no quake. So, what had awakened him?

"Jake," a voice said.

"Who's there?"

"Utz Seehafer."

When his sleep was disturbed, it could take Jake a long time to wake-up. He shook his head, trying to think. "You? Why are you here?"

Jake sucked in a sudden breath. *Am I about to be assassinated?*

"I'm here to take you to the Jewel Islands. Several colonies of *umjaadi* live near there," Utz said. "There's a spacecraft waiting outside for your team."

"What? Why?"

"Because my King commanded me to give you respect for your show on the fight floor today."

Jake grinned to himself. Their plan worked. This was a big concession.

But then, he groaned inwardly. So, they could go, but only if they took a spy with them, someone who could report back to the king.

What did that matter? They could do the medical research and go home!

"Get the others. Meet me on the rooftop. The spacecraft will be landing in fifteen minutes. Leave what luggage you can because it's a tiny craft."

THE SOUTH SEAS

January 16
The sunrise was swift.

Nearing the equator, Utz thought. In those latitudes, sunrise and sunset happened within minutes.

He reveled in the feel of the *Tokyo*, the spacecraft he'd named after the sound of Godzilla's roar. It was the smallest of the Bo-See fleet of ships, just a four-passenger, including the pilot. Ancel Fallstar handled most of the fleet, but this one was reserved for the king. Utz loved how well she handled. They were over water, not surprising since Rison was 80% water. On the horizon, a black plume spewed ash into the air, probably a new uncharted volcano.

Utz glanced back at his passengers. The three crew's seats reclined, allowing the adults to sleep while he flew. Jake was the odd man out, sleeping curled up on the floor. Not the best accommodations, but it worked.

Utz was excited about this mission. He believed it was important for the Earthlings to get what they needed. Since he planned to evacuate to Earth, this was an amazing opportunity to gain favor with important people. He didn't plan to go to Earth as a nobody. He might not become the King of the Bo-See, but he could be an important person among his people on Earth. If everything went well, it could change his future. If.

But it was going to be hard to ignore his natural dislike of them.

Jake had slept fitfully on the floor, and now he rubbed his eyes and scratched his scalp with both hands, as if that would clear his head. A few moments later, Jake stumbled forward to slump on the floor beside the pilot's chair.

Utz eyed him, and wondered again if they were doing the right thing. Would it give them any advantage on Earth like Dr. Mangot claimed?

"We're almost to the Jewel Islands," he said politely. "We'll land on Onyx Island, the largest. The islanders run a private resort, and right now, there's no one there. They'll welcome us. It's remote enough that no one will find us."

Suddenly, the communicator whistled. "Hello, *Tokyo*. Why are you flying south in this area?"

Jake leapt to his feet and peered out the windows, scanning for vessels.

Utz gulped. Fallstar's men. But he was ready.

"Hello. This is Utz Seehafer, Prince of the Bo-See. Who's speaking?"

Jake gripped the back of pilot's seat and watched Utz suspiciously. But Utz was confident he could take care of this.

"Alonso."

"Ah, skinny Alonso? Well, I'm just here to see about a woman."

A loud guffaw came from the speakers. "See about a woman? She's just a girl."

"Still," Utz said. His voice turned steely, and he said. "As is my right."

"Yeah, yeah. We just had to hail you and ask," Alonso said. "Give her a kiss for us!"

"*Tokyo* out," Utz said.

After a minute of silence, Jake released one hand and gestured. "What was that about?"

"The smugglers rule these waters. We chose this island because I have reasons to be here."

"A woman?" Jake was skeptical. "How old are you? 16?"

"17. Almost 18," Utz said.

"What? Are you getting married or something?"

But Utz refused to say any more, keeping his own counsel. He wasn't even sure that Mitzi Adams was still on Onyx Island. It was just a convenient excuse.

Jake went to the tiny galley, moving quietly to let the others sleep. He found a bottle of *wolkev* juice, and settled back beside the pilot's chair. Once he leaned forward and said, "What happened to our ship, the *Eagle 10*?"

"She's under the Prime Minister's control."

Jake frowned. "I'd be happier in the Earth ship."

"We'll be providing all the transportation you need."

Jake shook his head. "Including getting all of us up to the moon? How will you do that?"

"The *Tokyo* can take a big load."

After the initial shock, Jake calmed slightly. Utz smiled grimly. The Earth crew didn't like relying on the Bo-See for their safety. He didn't blame him, but it was the only way his father had been able to convince his leaders to allow this. The Bo-See had to be in control, always.

"This does seem to be a powerful ship," Jake conceded. "What kind of motor?"

Utz was glad for the change of topic. He shrugged and said, "Father and I like to tinker with motors. We always double the power on any auto or ship or craft we own. It's a good ship."

Jake nodded, but didn't push for more information.

Utz was grateful that he wasn't full of arguments or even just idle chatter. When there was a landmark, Utz pointed it out, Jake rose to his knees to peer out the window, and that was it. The Koloman Volcano. Danot Island.

Finally, he spotted the first of the Jewels. "Anjus," he said. "Next will be Berry-Berry. All the islands are named for precious gems."

One thing that Earth and Rison had in common was an identical periodic table. The elements and periodic table was the same on both planets, even if the names were different. Even the particular arrangement of elements that created gem stones was like Earth's stones. Anjus was amber in English. Berry-berry was beryllium. And so on. The largest island and their target was Oralee, or Onyx in English.

Waking the others, Jake told them they'd be landing soon on Onyx Island. He handed around more *wolkev* juice, and the Earthlings more or less woke up.

Utz paid them little attention, focusing now on landing his craft. Because the island had served for many years as a royal retreat, it had a helipad on the north side. The spacecraft was larger than most helis, but the landing pad would work well enough.

Finally, he powered down the *Tokyo* and turned to the Earthlings. He let Jake translate for him.

"Welcome to Onyx Island."

ONYX ISLAND

When they stepped out of the spaceship, Jake was amazed by the tropical foliage. He knew the names of a few from his childhood studies, but he hadn't realized that most grew huge here. Plants comparable to Earth's ferns might grow two or three feet tall in Tizzalura, but here, they were ten or twelve feet. The scale of everything dwarfed him.

Once off the spacecraft, Dr. Mangot stretched her arms high, reaching for the sun. "Ah, this is so much better than the Tizzalura climate."

Jake, though, turned to study the dark metal craft, which looked exactly like the Fewtrell Fighter's ship. This was a smuggler's ship, not a Quad-de ship. Apparently, it had been modified and had an extremely powerful engine. There might come a time when they were grateful for that.

The Jewel Islands were hot and humid. Jake let Utz take the lead, climbing the forest path to the top of a hill where they found a wide, shady trail. Behind them came Blake, Captain Bulmer, and Dr. Mangot.

"This goes to the Crown Jewel resort," Utz said. "The owner, Hideaki Adams, has known our family for years."

Jake understood. This resort was a getaway for Bo-See politicians, which meant the owner would be very discreet. If he was prone to gossip, he wouldn't have remained a favorite for them.

But the resort was empty. There were three large buildings with thatched roofs. The first was obviously the dining area and business offices. The others would be guest rooms. Nothing was boarded up or locked—what was the point on an island like this when the planet was about to blow up? No one was around, either.

"I'll have to visit the village and find Hi," Utz said. "See what's up."

Jake considered going with him, but thought that Utz knew the islanders, and they'd be more helpful when talking to him without Earthlings.

After Utz disappeared down a jungle path, Jake explored the resort, leaving the adults on lounge chairs on the shaded porch. At times like this, he longed for his friends David or Jillian, who would be excited to explore with him. The interior was cool, and the decor was restful—subdued, but tasteful colors, cool tile floors, and comfortable couches. It was designed to make you want to sit and rest. Jake could see why the Seehafers liked this place.

Beyond the spacious gathering room was a dining room with scattered tables. He peeked into the kitchen, and then went to another building to check out the guest rooms. Jake was surprised that the rooms were unlocked, but again, what was the point here on the island?

Each room held a king size bed and had a luxurious bathroom. This was a world-class resort. And it was empty.

Jake stopped at the window of one room and gazed out. They were at the top of a hill, so below spread a magnificent view of the ocean. The fact that this resort was forgotten brought home to Jake the coming disaster. No one had time right now for a vacation, a place to zone out and get away from the hectic pace of life. That was a joke. Right now, everyone was fighting for any kind of life.

He thought of the days when he told his teachers or parents, "I'm bored."

He realized now that was like throwing gold coins into a sewer. It was good that he had this wake-up call; he only hoped that he'd remember this years from now. He didn't want to become an old man, and wake up one day, and realize that he'd wasted half his life by complaining. He vowed he'd never complain again about an odd moment of idleness. Instead, he'd take joy in the possibilities of the moment. He'd live that moment fully.

Jake went back to the porches and murmured to dad, "Empty. No one."

Dad nodded. "Business has probably been pretty light for a couple years."

"So, they'll want our business—" Jake broke off, shaking his head. When the planet imploded, money would mean nothing.

PILGRIMS

From the path, they heard a girl's laughter. Utz came into view first, and the girl behind him was dressed in a turquoise sarong tied at her waist and a bikini top. Utz waved, and a moment later, Utz and the girl joined them on the porch.

THE VILLAGERS

Reluctantly, Utz left the Earthlings at the resort and took the familiar path through the jungle to the village. He and his twin brother Fritz had taken the path so many times before that he could've done it in his sleep. They vacationed here in the Jewel Islands as often as possible. Father was always busy with visiting politicians, so the boys had been free to run and play as they wanted. They often went to the village to find other kids. This time, though, he had to find Hideaki Adams, the owner of the island and resort.

Suddenly, he stopped short. A bush beside the path was blooming, a profusion of white blossoms giving off a sweet and spicy smell. He bent to a blossom and inhaled deeply. The *beche* bloomed year around on the island, and its smell brought back so many memories, some good and some painful. He forced himself to move on and soon came out of the trees just east of the village and abruptly stopped short. The white beach was so familiar, and so was the young woman building a sand castle. Mitzi Adams was only three the first time he watched her tiny hands pat sand onto a castle. He'd known her all his life and had held those small hands several times. She was as lovely as ever. His fiancée.

Ӭ   ᥫ

The first time Utz saw Mitzi Adams was when they were three-years-old. The Seehafers were staying at the Crown Jewel resort for a couple weeks. Her father owned the resort, and her sun-kissed golden hair set her apart from all the other dark-haired island girls. She and Fritz built a sand castle together. Mitzi refused to let Utz help; she only wanted Fritz.

Jealous and angry, Utz waited till the castle was built and then crashed through it, playing monster.

Mitzi ran away crying.

Meanwhile, Fritz had jumped on him in their first real fist fight.

After that, Utz found other island children to play with and left Mitzi and Fritz to themselves. They were inseparable that holiday and every holiday after that. Utz and Mitzi tolerated each other for Fritz's sake because Fritz desperately wanted them to be friends.

When the boys turned thirteen, and their father, King Seehafer, had announced Fritz and Mitzi were to be engaged, no one was surprised. The engagement party was lavish and full of merriment. They wouldn't be wed until they were both eighteen, but this sealed the alliances and gave King Seehafer control over the crucial Jewel Islands. They were in the middle of a growing trade route, and before the alliance, they had paid heavily for the Jewel Islands to be a refueling station for their ships. With this alliance, everything would be renegotiated.

However, only a week after the engagement, Fritz died in a cave when a quake dislodged a slab of the ceiling, and it crushed him. Mitzi and Utz mourned together, sobbing and clinging to each other at Fritz's funeral. With Dad so stoic, Utz had nowhere else to turn. He spent time with Mitzi, but when the grief subsided, he realized that he still didn't like her.

Then Dad did the unthinkable. He told Utz that he and Hideaki agreed: Mitzi would now betroth Utz.

Fritz wasn't gone but six months when another celebration was held. He remembered the binding ceremony, how Mitzi looked so forlorn as she walked down the aisle toward him. Wispy tendrils of hair framed her gaunt face, and fragrant *beche* blooms were woven into the braids. She was so achingly beautiful that he thought maybe everything would work out. He could spend a lifetime with someone so regal. Just as she stepped onto the dais, she slipped and almost fell. A look of fatigue passed over her face.

We should've waited longer, he thought. *It's too soon for her.*

But she brightened, and Utz thought it would be okay.

Hideaki was resplendent in a white and floral sarong; he was covered with *beche* flower necklaces and had *beches* in his own hair. Hideaki's big hand put Mitzi's small one into Utz's hand. Somehow, Utz got through the ceremony without embarrassing everyone.

But afterward the smell of *beches* always reminded him of Mitzi and how she looked up at him with bewilderment and quietly moaned, "You're not Fritz."

Yet another way he had failed his father.

໑ ໑

Utz walked softly until his shadow fell across the sand castle. "Hello."

Mitzi whirled with a bright expression. "You!" Her brown eyes widened with shock.

Utz winced. That expression meant she was unhappy to see him. Quickly, he explained, "I'm here on business."

Mitzi turned back to her sand castle and patted down one side. Without looking at him, she said, "We heard the Earthlings were coming to search for *umjaadi*. Why did you come?"

Utz said nothing. Instead, he sat in the sand beside the castle and watched her work in silence. As the minutes stretched, the peaceful surroundings penetrated, and he stretched out his legs and leaned back on his hands to enjoy the sun and wind.

Finally, she spoke: "Those are worthless starfish, you know."

With a sigh, he pulled his knees up and hugged them. Quietly, he explained, "But they hold the key to an illness in the Phoke, the Earthling race that lives in their oceans. We need the Phoke to be our allies."

Mitzi sat back on her heels, tilted her head and considered. "These Phoke, do they have gills and breathe water?"

"No," Utz said. "Different anatomy, but I'm not sure how. You'll have to ask Dr. Mangot or Captain Bulmer about that."

Now, Mitzi glared straight at Utz. "So, have you come for me? Are you taking me off-planet with you?"

Again, Utz winced. Her words stung. He should be here to rescue his fiancée, and of course, he didn't want her to die when the planet imploded. But he also didn't want to be tied to this engagement. Conflicting emotions swirled, and he wanted to run away, to avoid this confrontation forever. He forced himself to focus on the task at hand. Gruffly, he asked, "Where's your father?"

"Out fishing. Trying to catch a *mundy*."

Utz grunted his understanding. It was hard for him to ask her, but he needed help. "Could you, or your Dad, arrange for someone to bring us a basket of food? And can you come up and show me things in the kitchen so we can take care of ourselves?"

She hesitated.

Utz understood. The whole world was going to blow up soon. Why should she work when the beach and the water called her? And like him, she had no loyalty to this engagement.

But she agreed, "Yes."

They stopped at the village quickly for Mitzi to talk to a couple people. The houses had woven mat walls that rolled up to open to let in the wind. The thatched roofs made them blend in with the jungle foliage. She stopped another girl who was wearing a red bikini top and a sarong skirt, and quickly explained the supplies she needed. "Nola, could you bring them up to the resort?"

The girl wore an eye-patch, and when she saw Utz looking, she said, "Infection last month. We had nothing to treat it and no way to get anything. I'm blind in that eye now."

Utz's stomach gripped in sympathy, but it was a story he'd heard everywhere in the last six months. Medical problems were ignored because, well, in the face of utter destruction, an eye infection counted for little.

The girl nodded, and with arrangements made, they turned back to the path toward the Crown Jewel. Climbing the slope, side by side with Mitzi, he could almost imagine that he was Fritz, and this was how life had meant to be.

The Earthlings were all on the porch, resting in the deep shade. Spotting them, Jake stood immediately, impatient as always.

"We've got some things worked out," Utz said. He blinked in the darkness of the porch, his eyes taking a minute to adjust. "This is Mitzi Adams. Her father, Hi, owns the island." He hesitated, glanced at her, and then down at his bare feet. The tops were covered with white sand. "She's, um, my fiancée."

"Oh!" Jake said, obviously surprised.

Utz sighed. He'd almost said, "My brother's friend." She wasn't his friend. Never was. But officially, she was his fiancée.

Ignoring the curious looks, Utz forged onward. "They'll get us started, and they don't mind us using the resort. But no maids or cooks."

Utz introduced the team, who each stood up and shook Mitzi's hand—a very Earth-like gesture that embarrassed her. By Jake's turn, she had firmly placed her hands behind her back.

Jake just nodded and asked, "Is there any way we can get some breakfast? I'm starving."

Mitzi shrugged. "None of the villagers are interested in serving anymore."

Utz said, "If the islanders help us, it'll be out of kindness, not from any payment we might offer." He asked Mitzi again, "Do you mind showing me where things are?"

Mitzi looked at Utz and her face softened. "I'll help you."

She was staring at him with a raw yearning.

He'd seen that look on the face of people in Killia, a desperate grasping for life. Utz didn't like it, but they had to take advantage of Mitzi's interest in getting off-planet, because they had to eat while on the island.

Nola marched up the steps. She held a large basket that appeared to be full of food: pineapples, eggs, bread and more.

Jake gawked at the beautiful girl. Utz wanted to tell him that all the islander girls looked like this, but stopped himself. Why spoil a good surprise?

"Here, Mitzi." Her voice was low and melodic. Glistening dark hair fell like a waterfall to mid back while she moved gracefully. When she turned, though, so that Jake saw her eye patch, he gaped anew. Then, awkwardly, he looked away.

Mitzi turned and took the basket. "Thanks. Want to help me cook some breakfast for them?"

The girl shook her head. "Nah. Everyone else is going sailing. See you later."

She waved and turned away toward the beach path.

Mitzi shrugged and said ironically, "Hard to get good help these days."

Utz said, "We can cook for ourselves if you want to go sailing."

"No, I'll visit with you. Why don't you come in the kitchen and help?" She turned to the rest of the group. "Just pick out a room, we don't care. You won't have any maid service, but you're welcome to use the washing machine. Hmmm. If you want hot water, you'll have to fill the cistern and let the sun warm it up."

Jake shook his head. "It's OK. A cool shower will feel great."

An hour later, they gathered in the dining room, ready to make plans. Utz had explained to Mitzi that they needed to find a breeding pair of *umjaadi* starfish.

When they were all served a simple meal of fruit and cheese, Mitzi sat down with them to discuss the situation. "The seas are erratic now," she said. "You never know where a new vent will start pouring out magma. The water temperatures are already five to ten degrees above normal across the planet, with hotter spots here and there. Some marine animals can't take it. We've had massive die-offs of several species."

Dr. Mangot speared a piece of pineapple and leaned forward. "Do you know where the *umjaadi* did live? We could start there."

"I'll ask my father," Mitzi said. "He might know."

"Can we do that soon?" Dr. Mangot insisted.

"No, he's out fishing. He's always sworn that he'd catch a prize *mundy* fish, so he's been spending a lot of time on that."

At Jake's puzzled look, she added, "It's a popular sporting fish that can be taller than a man."

Utz swallowed. What things had he vowed to do before he died? Nothing really. He was just 14—startled, he realized that his birthday was on March 1, and he'd be 15. He couldn't blame Mitzi's dad for being so interested in something like catching a big fish. You should you fill your last days with family and friends and fishing.

Blake asked, "Are there boats we can use? Maps?"

"Sure, we can do that much," Mitzi said. "But we have little gasoline, so it's row boats or sail boats."

Captain Bulmer suggested, "Let's just go to the beach this afternoon, snorkel a bit and get our bearings. We'll check out the boats and gear so we can be out early tomorrow."

"We're moving too slow," murmured Dr. Mangot. But, with a shrug, she added, "Don't see how we can do it faster, though."

THE *UMJAADI* STARFISH

They spent the afternoon at the beach getting set up. Captain Bulmer and Mitzi checked out the available sail boats, while Utz swam and Blake snorkeled to get an idea of visibility and any other parameters that might affect their dives. Jake helped Dr. Mangot with chemical testing of the waters, an important data point for her research.

That evening, Utz took Blake and Jake along as he went looking for Hideaki Adams, the owner of the island resort. They needed more information on the *umjaadi* starfish, so they could plan their dives.

The village, a group of thatch-roofed houses, lay north of the resort. It was easy to find the villagers who were gathered around a bonfire on the beach. A whole animal—pig-like or calf-like—was roasting on a spit, and the smell was sharp and spicy. When they appeared in the firelight, a voice rang out, "Welcome!"

Immediately, a crowd of people pressed around interested in Blake, who was the first Earthling they'd seen.

"Raise up your arm," someone called. "We want to see if you have gills."

Blake just wore a tank top and shorts, so he obliged them.

"Oh! Hairy!"

Shocked, the crowd just stared until one brave girl pushed forward to touch Blake's hairy armpit, and then everyone wanted to.

Utz roared. "Hey! Give us room."

Laughter clamored around them and several reached in to pat Blake's shoulder.

"Hey! Give them room!" A bearded man, large and thick, broke through the crowd. Jake smiled in surprise. Tizzalurians rarely had beards, especially such a thick one.

Utz nodded at the man and said, "Let me introduce you to Hideaki Adams."

By flickering firelight, Hideaki looked nothing like his daughter. Where Mitzi was blond and fair, Hideaki was dark-haired and deeply tanned. Mitzi's personality was pleasant, but Hideaki looked vicious. Part of that was a dark tooth at the front of his mouth, but part of it was just his physical presence. He was obviously from Seehafer stock, so his body was thick and stone-hard. The biggest difference, though, was the respect he commanded. As soon as he called for people to back off, they did.

Jake stepped forward and said, "Sir, I am Jake Quad-de. Let me introduce Commander Rose, from the United States Navy, of the United States on Earth."

Blake stuck out his hand, so Hi shook it.

"Come and sit," Hi said. "We'll talk."

"Excuse me," Utz said. "I'll say hello to Mitzi and be right back." He nodded at the girl on the edge of the crowd.

They nodded and followed Hideaki to seaweed lounge chairs near the fire. Someone handed them cool drinks, a sweet fruit punch made from unknown fruits.

"How can I help you?" Hi said. He lay back on the lounge chair and closed his eyes.

Is he listening? Jake wondered.

Blake talked confidently, though, and Jake translated for him. "We are looking for the *umjaadi* starfish. We had one of the glow star globes, and it accidentally broke contaminating at least one waterway on Earth. It's caused a severe illness in the Phoke."

"I know that much," Hi said without opening his eyes.

"We'd like to catch a couple breeding pairs of the starfish," Blake said.

"Hmm. Do you think it will help?" Hi asked.

"No idea," Blake said. "But the Phoke doctor thinks it will."

"Female starfish are easy to catch. This time of year, you'll find them in about 50 feet of water anywhere off the islands." His voice was deep, gruff, and almost sounded like he was angry. "It's the males that are hard to find. They live deeper and only come up at night to find food. Since they are a dark maroon, almost black color, they are hard to see. It's like a black ghost fish in a black sea. The only time we manage to catch males is during spawning time when they join the females in shallow waters. For you, since you don't know our seas, it'll be impossible."

Impossible! Jake wished that Hi had lied to them, had allowed them to hope. They'd come so far—half a galaxy—to find a cure for the *umjaadi* illness. They were so close. And now, Hi dashed their hopes of finding the starfish quickly, if they could find it at all. If these islanders couldn't find the male starfish, how would they?

Jake could see now that they were fools on a fool's errand. They had expected to waltz into a foreign environment, grab what they needed immediately, and leave. Tasks were always more complicated than he expected.

"Is there any bait that would help? Could we entice the males up for a special food?" Jake asked.

Hi shrugged. "Not that I know of."

"Is there any way to herd them out of the depths?"

Hi snorted. "What? You want to send a *kyrra* down to chase them up?"

"Isn't there something we can try?" Jake asked, exasperated with Hi's answers.

"Not that I know of. Do you want me to say it again? Not that I know of. No one has ever cared about that starfish. It's not good to eat, and there's nothing different about them from a thousand other species of starfish, except they can survive in a closed environment like a glow globe."

Jake wanted to protest, to ask more questions, to find an answer. They had to catch a male starfish so Dr. Mangot could run the right tests. He didn't want to hear the word "impossible."

Dad said, "I guess we'll catch the females tomorrow. That will leave us time to find a way to hunt the males."

We're so close, Jake wanted to moan. But it would be as foolish as thinking you could embrace the distant moon. He could see success, but he couldn't touch it.

They would fail. Em would die.

For a moment, he contemplated a universe where Em no longer lived. No, that was the definition of "impossible."

But even the natives had trouble catching the male starfish.

Utz appeared frowning, and almost growled, "Do you have what you need?"

Blake looked up and blinked in surprise. "Yes."

"Let's go."

Apparently, Utz had argued with Mitzi. Jake shoved up to his feet, ready to leave the despair about catching a male starfish. He needed time to think about what this all meant, to find a way to squirm out of this difficulty.

"Wait." Hi sat up and glared at Utz. "I hear that you're going off-planet. You're taking Mitzi, right?"

Utz looked down and scuffed his feet in the sand.

Frantically, Jake recounted the people who had to board Utz's small spaceship. Oh, this was going to be bad.

Hi rose and stepped closer to Utz. "Because," he continued in a soft voice, "you're engaged. She's a priority for you. Right?"

Utz glanced up and took a step back at the threatening bulk. "Hi," he said, his voice pleading, "you know."

"Know what?"

Utz's voice broke. "I'm not Fritz."

Surprisingly, Mitzi was there to put a hand on her father's arm. "It's okay. I understand. I wouldn't go with him anyway."

Hi looked down at her and pulled her into a fierce embrace. They stood there for a long moment, father and daughter, grieving over the loss of their way of life.

Finally, Hi looked up and waved Utz away.

Utz turned and trudged off toward the resort. Blake and Jake followed.

When he caught up, Jake said, "What was that about?"

"None of your business."

Jake said, "Fritz. I think Swann said something about him. Was that your twin brother?"

Utz whirled around, fists up, ready to fight.

Jake skipped back and held up his hands in a peace gesture. "Okay. We don't have to talk about it."

THE FIRST SAIL

The next morning dawned hazy and smoggy, presumably from some distant volcano spewing ash into the air.

Mitzi surprised them by joining them on this first sail. She and Utz seemed to have a truce of whatever had caused the argument the night before. She didn't smile much, but she was efficient in helping get them on-board.

Captain Bulmer had chosen an older sailboat because he said she was more seaworthy than other vessels. She needed a new coat of varnish on her decks, but of course, no one was going to put the effort into that. The sails were relatively new and without patches as on other boats.

With Mitzi's help and advice, Captain Bulmer had the sails singing as they tacked out of the bay into open water. Captain Bulmer was tall, but not as tall as most Boadan sailors, so the tiller wasn't at a comfortable height. Still, it was doable, and besides, they only had a short sail to their destination. Just outside the bay entrance was one of the smaller, unnamed islands in the Jewel Island chain.

Despite differences from Earth's sailing boats—a different way of rigging the lines, a sharper keel and designed for taller people—she handled beautifully. Jake loved the way the ship cut through the waves and leaned into the wind. When they stopped and threw over an anchor, Jake was sad to stop sailing. But they had work to do.

Dad cheerfully pulled on his tank and mask, while Captain Bulmer just stripped to swim trunks. When Dr. Mangot came up from the cabin, Jake thought again that she'd probably been a stunning woman in her youth. But now, in a swimming suit, Dr. Mangot just looked middle aged. And tired. She wasn't holding up well under the stress of their mission.

Utz and Mitzi handed out nets attached to a long stick, and then Mitzi demonstrated how to twist the net at the last minute to scoop up the starfish. When everyone seemed clear on the nets, Utz and Mitzi dove in first, followed by the adults.

Jake was the last to jump in, and he reveled in his native seas. He bobbed back to the surface, but then he zipped his legs together and kicked underwater. The water was clear, with visibility up to twenty or thirty feet.

Warmth embraced him, and Jake captured a mouthful of water. Salty, of course, but a different flavor from the Gulf shores of Alabama or the cold Puget Sound waters. There was a freshness to the water, like it was, well, clean. Slowly he blew the water back out. He could swallow some without a problem, but he shouldn't drink lots of it because he wasn't a full-blood Risonian. His mom could swallow water all day without problems because she had a salinity gland to rid her body of the salts. It was part of the Risonian nose ridge system. It was also one of the things that Jake had failed to inherit. Still, it was a joy to taste his home waters again. It was like a favorite food rediscovered.

The shallows near the island brimmed with seaweed that hid small creatures. In several areas, the *umjaadi* female starfish clumped into small colonies. Jake used his net to scoop a starfish, letting the sand dribble away. He dropped it into a catch sack held by Utz and turned back to pick out another female. They wanted maybe a dozen breeding pairs.

Within thirty minutes, the team had captured a couple dozen starfish of varying sizes. Jake's largest one was a lighter maroon color, with brilliant yellow tips. The others were darker, almost black with the yellow-tipped legs. Utz said the lighter ones were healthier and kept releasing some of the almost black ones.

Jake scooped up another starfish when the planet shook. The starfish drifted out of his net, but Jake barely noticed.

The quake vibrated the water all around him, which probed his insides until he quivered all over. It was more disconcerting than a quake on land because on land, only the ground under your feet shook. Here, the world shook all around him. Though it wasn't a big quake, it still left Jake rattled. He'd been confident that they'd find the starfish and return quickly to Earth.

For the first time, he admitted the risks: *I may not get off the planet in time. I might die here.*

Heart pounding in a sudden panic, Jake whirled to check on Blake. The quake had shaken his scuba regulator out of his mouth, but he was calm enough to just grab it and return it to its place. Blake, the Navy man, wouldn't panic, even if Jake wanted to. Somehow, that steadied Jake.

They all paddled back to the boat—Jake desperately trying to control his shifting emotions. Of course, he should've expected that quakes would start coming faster and would build in intensity. He just hadn't thought about being underwater when it happened.

He heaved out onto the boat's deck which rocked gently with the waves. It was too similar to the quake's rocking, and it took Jake a minute to find his sea legs. The best of the netted starfish were placed into a dozen prepared glow star globes and sealed inside. It would be the easiest way to transport them, and they should be fine in the globes for a year or two.

Jake swiped his hands on his shorts and wished for a shower to remove all the ocean's salts from his skin. He hesitated, wanting to talk about the quake; he wanted to be reassured that, "Everything is fine."

Instead, he forced himself back to the business at hand, the only thing that could really get them off-planet faster. "Females are easy to catch. How will we catch the males?" he asked the team.

Dad, Captain Bulmer, Dr. Mangot, Utz and Mitzi just shrugged bleakly at him. They were all just as agitated by the earthquake as he was.

"We'll sleep on it," Dr. Mangot said. She looked even more tired, with dark circles under her eyes now.

Worried, Jake stepped forward, and before she could stop him, put his palm on Dr. Mangot's forehead. He frowned. "You're hot. You're running a temperature."

DAUGHTER OF TIZZALURA

Utz stepped off the lodge's porch barefoot, holding his shoes in his hands. He'd need them when he reached Marasca.

A voice startled him. "Where are you off to so early?"

Spinning, Utz located a shadow under the deep overhang of the porch. Jake was in a lounge chair.

"Marasca, if you must know," Utz said.

"What?" Jake sat up.

"I have to see someone," Utz said. He turned and walked toward the path.

Jake shoved up and strode across the porch. "When will you be back?"

Utz knew that Jake was worried about him taking the space craft and not returning. If he abandoned them, they'd be stranded—forever. "Don't worry. I'll be back. 24-36 hours at the most. Find those starfish. We need to get off-planet."

An angry growl erupted, and Utz glanced back over his shoulder. In the dark right before dawn, it was impossible to read Jake's facial expression. But his voice said that he wasn't happy.

Utz shrugged. It wasn't his job to make the Earthlings happy. He was becoming used to their ways, and he still needed to please them enough so they'd help him get established on Earth. But first, he had business to take care of. That quake yesterday had scared him; a deep worry was settling into his chest and making it ache.

Mitzi had pushed hard for him to take her to Earth, and she was right. They were engaged, which meant she was supposed to be his future. But she wasn't the future he wanted. They had bitter words that night on the beach, but in the end, they both knew it was never going to happen. She helped them search for starfish yesterday as an apology.

When she left them at the dock, the sun was glinting off the water. She stopped to touch his hand, and he looked up.

"Good-bye, Utz Seehafer." Her face was lit with the golden light, and she looked lovelier than ever.

He shook his head in sorrow. "Good-bye, Mitzi Adams."

There was so much more they both should've said. But after a moment of silence, she turned and trotted away down the beach.

He didn't expect her to help them again.

He didn't expect to see her again.

It was one more thing to mourn, but he didn't have time to do that, yet.

As they had fished yesterday, his plan had hardened in his mind, but he wasn't in a hurry to make it happen. The earthquake, though, and Mitzi's good-bye had finally shaken him out of his inaction. He woke this morning feeling the urgency and realized he had to do something right away. So, he was heading to Marasca and would make arrangements with his cousin Ancel Fallstar to smuggle Godzilla and Derry, as the shark's caretaker, to Earth. She had to make it off-planet. One last night in Marasca, the city of his childhood, wouldn't hurt either.

Utz laid in a course for Marasca, then set the ship to auto-pilot and set a timer for two hours. He'd wake up far enough outside of the city to bring it in manually.

Just as he'd planned, when he woke, the sun was just above the eastern horizon. The volcanic smog was so bad that he could only see a smudged pale-gold ball. He chewed his bottom lip and tried to decide where to land. He wanted to be secretive about this visit, but in the end, he realized it didn't matter. Worrying about gossip was pointless. He had little time, so he needed to be efficient.

He circled the city once and almost wanted to weep. The white marble city was beautiful, even with volcanic ash trying to obliterate every bit of white. The architecture was classic Risonian, with square edges, deep overhangs and exacting proportions that lent the city an elegant grace. The city climbed the slopes of a small hill, and at the top lay his father's palace, a prize wrested from the last incompetent ruler who fell beneath his father's knife on the fight floor. Utz had lived there for the last three years and made many fond memories playing in the palace and the city.

But today, he needed Derry, not his father.

Utz landed the space craft in a green area beside the bay where the great white sharks swam. He leapt out, locked the doors and strode toward the laboratory. When he entered the lab, his knees went weak at the sight of Derry, sitting on a stool and looking into a microscope.

She looked up, and her face lit up, bright eyes glowing. "You came back."

Utz was beside her instantly. Soberly, he said, "I came back for you."

ꚃ   ꚃ

Utz helped Derry out of the hover car, watching as she put her good foot down first and heaved upright. When she was steady on her feet, he tucked one of her hands into his elbow and led her forward at a stately pace. The palace was beautifully and tastefully lit with soft downlights that created a calm, peaceful cocoon around the gardens.

"You're sure I need to meet him?" Derry asked. Her face was pinched with concentration as she tried to walk without limping.

Utz pulled her a bit closer. "No, you don't *need* to meet him. I *want* you to meet my father. Just as in happier days, I'd insist that I meet your father."

She nodded and tried to pull herself even straighter. Instead, her foot caught on her skirt and she tripped, almost falling except for Utz's support.

Utz wished he could turn and run away from this meeting. But Seehafers didn't avoid something just because it was difficult.

Guards smoothly opened the front door. Utz wondered if they'd be loyal to the King right up to the end. Habit was carrying most people through these last days.

Utz and Derry swept through the front hall and into the library. It was just after lunch time; Utz had carefully planned this so he'd find his father reading alone, as he always did after eating.

King Seehafer turned from the fireplace and shut down the book on his view screen. "Utz! I thought you were in the Jewels."

Then he caught sight of Derry. "Oh. Hello."

Derry curtsied, careful to maintain balance.

Utz said in a stony voice, "Father, I present Derry Rudak, daughter of Professor Raymond Rudak, Tizzalurian professor of linguistics." She had no titles, but he had to add something to her name.

King Seehafer stepped forward and took her hand. "Greetings. It's not often I meet a daughter of Tizzalura." Tilting his head and looking from one to another, he asked, "Why are you in Marasca?"

Derry looked sideways at Utz, and at his nod, she said, "I'm studying comparative anatomy at Marasca U. Utz offered to show me the great white sharks from Earth. That's how we met. Did you know that the male had—when I counted—about 3200 teeth?"

Utz cleared his throat.

Derry looked crushed and apologized, "But you don't need to hear that. I'm sorry, sir. I get enthusiastic."

King Seehafer chuckled, "No, it's interesting. Tell me more."

"This isn't the right time," she protested.

"Did the female have the same number?"

"Only 2800. But she's smaller. Weighs about 12% less than the male. I don't know if that's normal, or they're just different here on Rison for some reason."

The King looked up at Utz, amused. "I see why you like her."

Utz froze. Did Father really like Derry, or was he just toying with him? Either way, he forced the words out. "Yes, I do like her. I'm taking her with me to Earth."

The King froze. Groping behind him, he reached for the sofa and sat. "You've decided. You're leaving."

Utz knelt and took his father's hands. "Yes. I must. I want a future."

King Seehafer stared at his son without really seeing him. "But Fritz is here."

"No. Fritz is gone." Had been gone for months, and still whenever Father saw Utz, he really saw Fritz.

Utz's head lamp shone on his twin brother, Fritz, who lay on the cave floor shivering. Frantic with fear and worry, Utz pulled off his jacket and laid it over Fritz.

Hurry, Father! Hurry! He wanted to shout.

They'd come underground to gather water samples from the large lake that lay under the hillside. Scientists had been gathering samples every month for a decade now, and tracking the chemicals seeping into the water to see how it was affected by increased volcanic activity. He and Fritz had turned thirteen last week, and Father decided to take them along.

It had been exciting to dress in boots, warm clothes and headlamps. Fritz flashed the lights around their hover car until Dad was irritated and made him stop.

They were nearly identical twins, physically hard to tell apart, and often thought the same things. But Fritz was first born, which meant he naturally got more attention. In the Bo-See, first-born inherited and that meant everything. Utz had always been secretly glad he was second-born because he wasn't constantly scrutinized.

Naturally, Fritz went first, leading the way into the cave. Utz felt a swell of pride in his brother. When they returned, they'd have something to brag about to their friends and classmates.

"Slowly," Father said. But he let Fritz choose their path through the jumbled rocks.

The journey down, away from the light and into the bosom of the mountain, was thrilling but uneventful.

At the lake, Utz flashed his light across the water and couldn't find the opposite shore. Father said it took thirty minutes to row across, that he'd done it several times in search of scientific information. In the end, though, scientists had been content with water samples. Tracking the water across time, the sulfur content had gone up, and the mean water temperature had risen five degrees. The planet's unstable core was there in the data.

Father recorded the water's temperature—the highest so far—and tucked several vials of water samples into his backpack. Finally, he nodded for Fritz to lead the way back to the surface.

And that's when the quake struck.

At first, the floor just trembled as if a shiver of fear had run down its spine. Utz froze, looking upward and shining his light onto the cave's ceiling. Their passage was wide and smooth. Suddenly, everything heaved and bucked in slow motion, as if a giant serpent was passing beneath. Just as suddenly, he found himself in a heap on the ground, with his heart pounding. The cave floor was still, but dizziness swept over him in waves.

"Fritz, are you OK?" Father called. "Utz?"

"Fine," called Utz.

Fritz only moaned.

Quickly, Father and Utz located Fritz. He lay under a large slab of rock that had sheared off the ceiling. Together, they heaved the rock aside.

Fritz lay with his leg at an odd angle, obviously broken.

Horror struck Utz, and he sat abruptly to put his head between his knees to keep from throwing up.

Fritz moaned and tried to put his hands to his head. "What happened?"

Feeling the nausea pass, Utz looked up.

Father felt Fritz's leg and winced. "Not good. I'll have to get help." He looked at Utz. "Can you stay with him while I go to the surface and call for a medical team?"

Utz nodded. "Of course," he said hoarsely.

"Here," Father said, shrugging off his backpack. "I have some first-aid supplies." He shook his head and wiped a dirty streak across his eyes. "We should elevate his head, but I'm afraid he's got a concussion, too. Keep him warm. Put your jacket over him and lay beside him. Keep him warm."

Father bent to run the back of his hand across Fritz's forehead. "Keep him warm. I'll be back as fast as I can."

Father's flashlight bounced away, his boots thumping and echoing against the cave's hard walls.

Almost frantic with fear, Utz stripped off his jacket and lay it across Fritz. He lay beside him, as close as he dared, afraid to hug him lest he injure something else. I should turn off my light and conserve the battery, he thought.

But he shivered just thinking about waiting in the dark. What if there was another quake?

Father hadn't thought of that! Should he try to carry Fritz and get closer to the entrance? But Fritz weighed too much for him. They both were a throwback to the old body type of their ancestor Utz Pharomond, squat, short, and muscular.

Fritz was shivering.

"Keep him warm," Father had said. But how?

"Utz," Fritz's voice was weak.

"I'm here."

"You'll have to be the heir now."

"What? No. You're going to be OK."

Fritz groped for Utz.

Utz took his brother's hand in his own. Fritz's hand was so cold!

"Make Father proud. For me."

"No, no, you'll be fine." Tears streamed down Utz's face.

"Promise me."

"Of course, I promise. But it's crazy; you'll be fine." Fritz had to be fine. Because there was nothing without his brother, his other half. "I promise," Utz whispered. "Just stay with me."

The medical team arrived three hours later. Utz's flashlight had long since gone dead. For endless hours and days and years and eons, he had sat in the dark and cradled his twin brother and tried to keep him warm.

And failed.

It was bad luck, they said. If they'd been able to get there in fifteen minutes, Fritz might have had a chance because his injuries weren't that bad. Lying there in the cold and without treatment, though, he went into traumatic shock, and that's what killed him.

It was just an accident, they said. No one could predict that a quake would strike while they were underground. No one could have predicted the chaos from the quake that would prevent help from coming quickly.

It's not your fault, they said.

When they took Fritz away, Utz stared at his father's back. He crouched over the place where Fritz had died and cried. He raised his eyes to the rock ceiling and cried out his anger and grief.

Utz huddled against a wall, just watching. Alone.

When Father finally came to himself, he stood and looked around. His eyes found Utz, but they were empty. He shook his head, and wiped the back of his hand across his eyes. He stammered, "F-F-Fritz?"

Utz could only whisper his name, "Utz."

Father grimaced and shivered. "Utz, not Fritz."

The words echoed in the cave tunnel, an angry snarl that wound around Utz until he covered his head with his arms, as if the words were pummeling him.

Silence. Peering through his arms, Utz watched his father.

Father stood silent for long moments, eyes closed, fists clenched. Then, without a word, he turned and trudged toward the cave entrance.

Utz almost stayed there. Alone. Where he wouldn't have to see that look in his father's eye. Every time Father saw Utz, he'd see instead the son he'd lost.

But Utz had promised his brother. Promised! The only thing he clung to was that promise. He would make his Father proud of him—for Fritz's sake.

But how? He wasn't Fritz and never would be.

It had been a hollow promise.

༰   ༰

Father looked at Utz and Derry. Suddenly, he stood, gripped Utz's forearms, pulled him closer, and stared. "Utz," he whispered.

"Yes, I'm here."

"You're Utz. And you have a future."

"Yes," Utz whispered, guilt stinging his eyes because he wasn't Fritz.

"You and—" he glanced at Derry, but apparently, he couldn't think of her name. He waved at her.

"Me and Derry," Utz said gently. "We're going to Earth."

Father dropped Utz's arms and leaned back, slumping against the sofa pillows. "Yes. You should go."

Utz licked his lips, hating that he couldn't just rush away, that he had to ask the next question. "Will you help us?"

Father roused himself and sat up. "What do you need?"

"I need to negotiate with Ancel Fallstar to smuggle Godzilla to Earth. Derry goes along as Godzilla's caretaker."

Father nodded slowly. "Good plan. Derry's leg—I'm sorry, but I couldn't help but notice. Well, it's a good plan."

"Will you pay Fallstar whatever he asks?" Utz held his breath. He had no way to pay and Ancel would demand thousands of US dollars, Indian rupees, or Japanese yen. But surely Father had reserves in Earth currencies.

"What?"

Utz repeated carefully. "Ancel will want the same fee for taking the shark pup to Earth as he did for bringing the pair of great whites here. Will you pay him for me?"

Before he even finished speaking, Father was shaking his head. "No. You pay your own way. No."

"Father." A lifetime of frustration spilled over into Utz's voice. "You know I have nothing because I'm so young. And these are different times. Traditions don't matter now, only survival. Please, give me—give us—a future."

The King rose and paced back and forth before the fireplace. "No, no, no," he murmured to himself. "They have to earn their fortunes, just as you did." He shook his massive head and argued with himself. "But there's no time."

In the Bo-See kingdom, family money was never inherited until after a person turned thirty-five or forty years old. It forced young men to work for their living and to find their own way. Utz saw the wisdom in it. But the planet's pending destruction changed everything.

Finally, King Seehafer threw up his hands and turned to Utz. "No."

Utz froze, holding his father's gaze. He desperately wanted to be angry with his father, to be bitter with rage. Instead, he understood. King Pharomond Seehafer was a Bo-See, through and through. He couldn't leave Rison because he'd be lost in a foreign society. Utz had to leave and take nothing with him. He was on his own.

"I'm sorry, Fritz," he thought. "I'll never make this man proud of me."

He nodded to the King—to his father—in understanding.

The King's jaw twitched, but he held himself rigid.

Utz turned his back on his father. He tucked Derry's hand into the crook of his elbow. Slowly, Utz and Derry walked away without looking back.

FISHING

Before Jake could even wake properly, Utz was gone. A few minutes later, he saw the space craft lift off and speed east. Jake groaned to himself. They were stranded and at the mercy of that crazy Seehafer.

With a shrug, he decided to go down to the beach, find a paddle board, and swim out to the island where they found starfish yesterday afternoon. No one seemed to know the habits of these starfish. Maybe the males and females got together at dawn. He shrugged. In any case, a morning swim would do him good.

But first, he stole into Dr. Mangot's bedroom to check on her.

Captain Bulmer had dragged a lounge chair from the porch to her room and now dozed beside her. His eyes popped open at Jake's entry. Instantly, he put a finger to his mouth to keep Jake quiet.

He turned back to Dr. Mangot and scrunched his face in concern.

Jake turned away, embarrassed by the show of emotion.

Captain Bulmer stood, light on his feet, and tiptoed to the door, pushing Jake outside.

"What?" Captain Bulmer said.

"Just checking on her. Is her fever still high?" Jake asked.

"Yes," Captain Bulmer said. "But she's about due for more antibiotics. She told me it might take 24 to 48 hours before the fever broke."

"So, she's doing as well as expected," Jake said.

Captain Bulmer shook his head. "No, she needs to get well. You don't understand how important she is to our people. She can't just die."

Jake was puzzled by his passion. "She volunteered to come, knowing that she might get sick."

"And I wish I was the one sick, not her," Captain Bulmer said. "It's hard to watch someone you l—" He stopped himself. Then squared his shoulders and said again. "It's hard to watch someone you love when they're sick."

Jake stepped back and crossed his arms against the raw emotion. "Ah, yes. Hard."

"What did you want to tell me?" Captain Bulmer said.

"I'm going to the dock to fish for breakfast. Do you need anything before I go?

Captain Bulmer rubbed a hand over his face. "Can you give me 5 minutes to clean up a bit?"

Jake nodded. "Sure. I'll sit with her for a few minutes."

Captain Bulmer went toward his room while Jake went inside and perched on the edge of the lounge. Dr. Mangot's breathing was loud, and her face was pink with fever. He found himself breathing in time with her breaths.

This is what Em was like when she was sick, he told himself. They hadn't allowed him to be there. Maybe that was part of his problem with Captain Bulmer's emotions. Because he'd been robbed of the opportunity to watch over Em while she was sick. Even now, he longed to be with her, to hold her up and support her as she walked. He wanted to warn her to slow down so she wouldn't relapse. Instead, he was here on Rison watching Dr. Mangot.

Jake suddenly wanted to know how sick she was. Touching the thermometer to her forehead, it read 102F degrees. Still too hot. Her face was flushed. She'd braided her thick hair, but tiny tendrils escaped and curled around her face, giving her an oddly girlish look.

Captain Bulmer came in quietly. He'd changed into fresh clothes, washed his face and combed his hair. He'd be competent and efficient as Dr. Mangot's nurse.

Jake stood and crept to the door. He whispered, "I'll bring you some breakfast when it's ready."

Captain Bulmer nodded without looking. Instead, he held Dr. Mangot's hand in his and watched her face. Jake left and shut the door quietly behind him.

The sun was barely over the horizon when Jake walked down to the beach. Mitzi was on the dock fishing, so he went out and leaned on the rough wood, chin in hands, to stare at the water. Crystal clear, the bay was teeming with fish.

"What are you trying to catch?"

She shrugged. Her blond hair was curling in the humidity. She wore a white t-shirt with a red swimming suit under it, and ragged shorts. Barefoot, she was tanned and beautiful. It was tempting to flirt with her.

But she wasn't Em.

He looked away, remembering how Em looked so intense right before a swim meet, her hair squished into a swim cap and her dark eyes flashing.

"Fishing for breakfast," Mitzi said. She spoke in English, and her command of the language was good, even if it did have a heavy Risonian accent.

Jake could've answered in a Bo-See dialect, but replied in English because that's what she'd chosen. "Good idea. Got another pole?"

She nodded toward a shack and said, "Take what you like."

Jake was back soon with a pole and some lures. But Mitzi handed him a worm instead.

"Lures are for when you're out deep. Here, they like something wiggly."

Jake nodded his thanks, baited his hook and dropped it in. The fishing poles were just poles with a long line and a bobber. Not the fancy rod and reels that Jake had seen on Earth. It was all they needed here.

"So, what's up with you?" Mitzi asked. "You haven't come by the village to meet anyone."

"We've been busy," Jake said.

"You're a Quad-de. The girls would be glad to meet you."

Jake was embarrassed. He knew his name would interest some girls, but not the kind of girls that would interest him. Jake shrugged. "Oh. Well, I've got a girlfriend."

"A human? You went off-planet and found someone?" Her voice was ironic. "All the good ones here, and you gotta go for a human." She shook her head.

Jake didn't want to get into an argument about where he chose friends, so he said nothing.

Her line jumped. She pulled in a small orange fish and said, "It's a good one to pan fry. I just need a couple more."

Jake nodded and jiggled his own bait.

Mitzi baited her hook again, stepped away a couple feet, and dropped the line again.

"You know, I left here when I was eleven," Jake said evenly. "I'm fourteen, almost fifteen. When I left, I didn't even know girls existed."

"Oh, Quad-de, we know what you are. You were always destined to have a human girlfriend."

Jake gulped. She was right. Probably everyone on Rison knew that Swann was only his step-father. When they saw Blake, it was obvious to everyone but Earthlings that Blake was his father. They'd never tried to hide it. But it had never been obvious to Jake that he had to wind up with a human girlfriend.

"How's the fishing?" Captain Bulmer stood at the edge of the dock.

How much had he heard? Did he suspect that Jake was half human? Had Dr. Mangot told Captain Bulmer about Jake's parentage? She'd sworn to tell no one, but she was very close to Captain Bulmer. It was a secret that had to stay a secret, especially when they returned to Earth.

Jake shrugged. "Nothing. How's Dr. Mangot?"

"I gave her the morning dose, and she went back to sleep. I won't leave her long, but I just needed some fresh air," said Captain Bulmer.

Mitzi's line jerked again. With a quick flip, another orange fish flopped on the dock, this one bigger. "That's enough for me," she said brightly. "I'll take these home and cook breakfast now."

She handed her pole to Captain Bulmer, then walked away briskly toward the village.

Captain Bulmer watched her go. "Did you make her mad?"

"She's always mad," Jake said.

"What did that mean? 'We know who you are.'" Captain Bulmer was watching him curiously.

From the bucket that Mitzi had left, Jake pulled out a skinny, black worm and handed it to him. While he threaded the worm onto the hook, Jake thought about what to say. He had to trust that Dr. Mangot was keeping her word. And that the fever didn't loosen her tongue.

"I'm a Quad-de," he finally said. "That doesn't mean much on Earth or in Aberforth Hills. But here—" He waved a hand. "—it's sort of like we're royalty." He gave Captain Bulmer a rueful grin. "The Quad-des have been in Tizzalurian politics for centuries. I could have my pick of any of the native girls."

Jake casually looked up to see the effect of his words.

Captain Bulmer squinted and looked Jake up and down. When he spoke, his Scottish accent was heavier than usual. "There's more to it than the Quad-de name. I can't quite figure it out. Yet."

Jake's stomach churned at Captain Bulmer's suspicions.

Captain Bulmer turned to drop his line off the dock. Instantly, he got a hit and pulled up a big orange fish.

Jake said, "Looks like you know what you're doing."

Captain Bulmer said, "Do you know what you're doing?"

It was a challenge to explain more about Tizzalurian politics, Jake's position on Earth, and maybe even the truth about his parents. But he wasn't talking to this Phoke.

"Apparently, not. I've been here fishing for half an hour and caught nothing."

By now, Captain Bulmer's hook was baited again. Instantly, he got another hit. The fish was smaller, but large enough to keep.

Jake pulled up his hook to find that the worm was gone. Something had stolen his bait.

He leaned on the dock and let Captain Bulmer fish instead. He wondered what Captain Bulmer was thinking. Did he suspect the truth, that Jake was a test-tube baby? Or did he think Swann was his real father? Or was he suspicious about something else? Angrily, he shook the thoughts. None of it mattered if they couldn't get off-planet.

Captain Bulmer broke into his thoughts. "That's five. Enough for breakfast?"

Jake nodded. "Thanks. Apparently, I'm not much of a fisherman. Let's see if I'm a cook."

They climbed the hill to the resort. Jake went to the kitchen to cook while Captain Bulmer went back to check on Dr. Mangot.

While Utz was gone, Jake had plenty of time to think. He'd grown up and changed so much since the day he first landed on Earth and visited Gulf Shores. He'd been defiant and gone swimming with the great white shark. Bainbridge High School had been an education, and he didn't mean what schoolteachers meant when he said that. He'd just learned about life and about himself.

Em had given him a different type of education, especially when he followed her to Aberforth Hills. And now, he was here in the south seas of Rison searching for a cure for her.

Through it all, he was the one who'd changed: from insecure to more confident, from naïve to wiser, and from socially inept to some level of social grace. He'd learned about his Earth family and his Rison family, and learned to appreciate and love them both. He couldn't imagine life without both.

But it was all for nothing if they couldn't find the male starfish and find the cure for Em.

They spent the next two evenings in fruitless dives. No matter how deep they dove, they never saw an *umjaadi* male. The island's daily temperatures soared, and the breeze was stagnant. When it did freshen some in the evenings, it always carried the sulfurous smell of volcanoes and ash. The planet shook—mostly small tremors—morning, noon and night. Time was short, and Jake chaffed that Utz was still gone.

SMUGGLER NEGOTIATIONS

Utz stood before a large sailing ship that flew the feared yellow flag of pirates. He smiled ironically to himself. It used to be a plain yellow flag, but after learning about Earth's pirates, Fallstar had taken to yellow flags with a skull-and-crossbones added. It was ironic how much they'd copied Earth.

Derry had wanted to come along, but since she was Tizzalurian, she didn't understand the Bo-See ways. Utz had to do this visit by himself.

At the ship, he called, "Permission to come aboard."

A tall Boadan man turned. He wore a wide-brimmed hat, but otherwise wore the yellow uniform that loosely proclaimed him a pirate. "Who's asking permission?"

"Utz Seehafer, Prince of the Bo-See, and cousin to the captain." He had many other ceremonial titles, but thought that was enough.

"Hmpf," the man said. Casually, he walked to the door of the captain's cabin and knocked. "Utz Seehafer to see you, sir."

The door flung open, banging against the cabin's front wall. "Utz!" A man dressed in scarlet—Ancel, himself—strode down the gangplank to Utz and buried him in a hug.

Utz flinched but allowed the hug. He tried not to remember when he'd sailed with Ancel. But it was hard to forget. He'd been thirteen and a half, and Father had insisted that since Fritz was gone, Utz had to learn everything about the Bo-See.

After an awful week of sailing, Ancel had hauled him into the palace and threw him onto the floor in front of his father. Fortunately, they were alone in father's library.

With disgust, Ancel said, "He's a Seehafer through and through. Are you sure you have any Boada blood in you?"

Father's face was cold marble, masking his fury. "What happened?"

Ancel laid it on thick: "First, this crybaby got seasick. A Boada getting seasick? Never."

Utz cowered on the rugs in shame.

Ancel continued smoothly, "And then, when we ran down to the south pole, he stood watch and almost got us killed by an iceberg that he didn't see. Then he had the gall to complain about guard duty because his fingers were frozen, and when the doc checked, the silly boy had let frost bite set in."

Utz climbed awkwardly to his feet and tried to speak, hoping to explain that he was trying to do his duty as watchman, and if he'd gone in to tend to his fingers, the sailors would've just laughed.

But the King motioned him to silence.

Ancel's voice boomed as he continued, "With great joy, we did our annual hunt of the mighty *kyrra* and found a massive one, twice the size of our boat! I've not seen the like in years. Still, we gave your son the honor of the lead harpoon. Not only did he miss, but he hadn't strapped the harpoon to his wrist, and he lost it. My best harpoon! Gone! Because of this incompetent imbecile."

"Enough!" roared Father, suddenly transforming to King Pharomond Seehafer writ large. "Say no more, or—"

Ancel nodded with satisfaction. "Now I have your attention. I'll take 2500 *nobbles* for the equipment lost and for the catch that he cost us."

With barely controlled fury, the King nodded curtly. He grabbed a small paper from his desk, scribbled on it, and handed the chit to Ancel. "You're a bloody thief," he said. "Hand that to the exchequer at the royal treasury, and he'll pay you. On your way out."

Suddenly, everything was calm again. How did Father do that? Utz wondered. He went from absolute fury to good-natured teasing in an instant.

When the door closed behind Ancel, the King rounded on Utz, arm raised ready to back-hand him. But there was a flash of something in his eye, and the hand dropped.

Fritz. He's thinking of Fritz, Utz realized. He wants to punish me, but I look too much like my dead brother. So he couldn't do it.

Father would never say the words to Utz, but they both knew. That Fritz would never have been seasick. That Fritz would've buried that hideous sharp harpoon into the great beast. That Fritz would have made Father proud.

Utz felt like a harpoon had pierced his heart. He was supposed to learn from his Boadan kin, and instead, he'd embarrassed his father and cost him 2500 *nobbles*. He was a failure.

♊ ♋

Gently removing Ancel's arms from his shoulders, Utz straightened and defiantly faced his cousin.

I'm trying, he called silently to Fritz's spirit. *I'm trying.*

Utz had to make one more effort, though. He didn't know what the future would hold, but he knew that he wanted a future. He'd do everything he could to get off planet, and once on Earth, do everything he could to help his people. Utz was going to Earth, and somehow he'd do something that would make his father proud. Father wouldn't go to Earth, that was clear. Utz knew, though, that with every task, every decision, he'd always be evaluating whether Father would approve.

Now, Ancel pulled him up the gangplank and into his cabin. "To what do I owe the honor of this visit, young prince? We thought you were busy entertaining the Earthlings."

With an inward moan, he realized that he should have expected that comment. Ancel and his father's other counselors had agreed to allowing the aliens to visit the Jewel Islands.

"Earthlings entertain themselves," Utz said curtly.

Looking around the captain's cabin, Utz was impressed. The luxuries of a hundred cultures had wound up here in a jumble of color and textures: rugs, paintings, objects such as vases and candlesticks, and much more. Apparently, Ancel was a collector.

Ancel said, "How are the Earthlings doing on their search for *umjaadi*?"

Utz shrugged. "Females were easy to catch. But the males are nocturnal and live quite deep. Besides, there are a couple new lava vents near Onyx Island, so the water temperature has killed off some areas. But I'm here on business," Utz said. "I want something smuggled to Earth."

Ancel's eyes lit up. "Business!" He clapped his hands and a young girl appeared. He gestured to her and said, "This is my daughter Diamond. She's learning the trade and will negotiate for me."

Diamond was a fiery young thing, maybe ten years old. She hadn't yet started growing into womanhood, so she almost looked like a boy. Red-headed, like everyone in their family, she wore a single braid down her back. Ancel's daughters were named for jewel stones: Sapphire, Ruby, Onyx, Emerald, and Diamond.

Utz frowned. This wasn't the time to train a smuggler how to negotiate. It was time to evacuate this planet.

Diamond squeaked, "We smuggle anything, anywhere in the universe. What did you have in mind?"

Now Utz laughed. "When did you start smuggling to 'anywhere in the universe'?"

Ancel's eyes wrinkled in mirth. Utz frowned. He hadn't remembered those wrinkles in his cousin's face. The last few years had aged him, as it had all their leaders.

"We've been smuggling across the universe since my daughters started wearing red," Ancel said, "and making regular runs back and forth to Earth."

That startled Utz. "Your daughters are piloting their shuttles to and from Earth?" When they'd appeared at the negotiations at the Quad-de estate, they'd worn the Fallstar scarlet, too. He shot a glance at Diamond, who also wore the Fallstar scarlet. "Does she fly spaceships?"

Diamond stepped forward now and put her hands on her slim hips. Boldly, she declared, "I am the negotiator for this transaction. Now, what do you want smuggled."

With a sign, Utz described what he wanted. "Last year, your father smuggled two great white sharks from Earth. Do you remember? Well, they bred and have a pup. I want that pup taken back to Earth, along with its caretaker."

"Why?" Diamond asked.

The question startled Utz. She should only care about the exchange of money—which he still didn't have—not about his reasons for shipping a baby shark across the galaxy. He thought for a moment about how to explain it in a way she could understand.

Finally, he said, "The Phoke, Earth's aquatic people, are getting sick from the *umjaadi* starfish. But the sharks and their pup aren't sick, even though there are *umjaadi* starfish in their enclosed bay. The pup is unique because he's an Earth creature, but he was born on Rison. He's a living petri dish of our oceans, their doctor would say." He shrugged. "Who knows? He might be an advantageous specimen in their research."

Utz didn't say it, but he also thought the pup might be a good surprise to have in reserve. It might be very valuable to someone whose son or daughter was sick. Utz might not have learned to sail from Ancel, but he had learned how to twist something to an advantage. It was far-fetched, but right now all he had were long shots. He certainly couldn't say he wanted the shark pup so Derry would have a good excuse to go to Earth.

Diamond absently rubbed her thumb and forefinger together. "Two passengers and one of them takes up almost all the room on one of our ships. People are desperate to get off Cadee and on their way to Earth. We could sell that space ten times over." She looked up and smiled easily, giving Utz a glimpse of the beauty that would come when she matured. She continued, "But you're family. Of course, we can do it for you. There's just the matter of price."

Utz tried to keep his face calm and neutral. "My Father has agreed to pay whatever you ask."

Ancel interrupted and held out his hand, "You have his chit, his note promising to pay?"

Utz grimly shook his head.

Ancel frowned. "No chit and only your word? No. Get us that chit or there's no deal."

Utz glared back at Ancel. "There's no time."

"So, Pharomond didn't agree. Then what do you have to bargain with?" He waved at Diamond to continue.

Utz's shoulders seized up in frustration, and he had to roll his shoulders to loosen them. Fury threatened to overwhelm him. He must get Derry up to the moon. At any price.

Diamond took a step closer and said, "Let me make this easy for you. Instead of our usual fees, I want that space ship you're flying."

"No!" This little girl wanted his spaceship? Impossible!

Diamond's grin spread, and she could barely stay still. "Very well. I'm sorry to say that our ships are full at the moment. We can't do business after all."

With a dignity beyond her years, she stomped off to stand on tiptoe at a porthole and pretend she was watching something.

Utz appealed wordlessly to Ancel, but he just grinned and waved Utz back to Diamond.

Utz fumed at himself. His outburst had cost him any bargaining position. Diamond had guessed correctly that the spaceship would be his pain point. Now, he could bargain all day and night, and Diamond wouldn't budge. After all, she'd learned negotiation from a master.

He didn't want to give up that ship because it was his backup evacuation plan. He couldn't carry much, but he and Derry could escape on it. It was large enough and sturdy enough to make it to the Cadee Moon Base anyway. Without it, he would have to depend on the Tizzalurian, Swann Quadde, to keep his promise to send a spaceship to rescue the Earth crew.

"I have to get back to the Onyx Islands," Utz protested.

Diamond turned back slightly and shrugged. "Of course, I can drop you off."

"The ship is called the *Tokyo*. I named her after an Earth myth about large creatures in Japan. The most famous monster was Godzilla, and it lived near *Tokyo*. Her spirit inhabits our spaceship. You wouldn't want a cursed spaceship."

"*Tokyo*! How quaint! I like it."

Utz screwed up his face at Diamond's enthusiasm.

She came to pat Utz's shoulder. "I'll take good care of her, you know."

"How old is Diamond?" Utz asked Ancel. He couldn't keep the anger from his voice.

"Twelve." Ancel smiled, his white teeth gleaming. "We start our smugglers young. Ah, if only I'd had you when you were twelve instead of thirteen."

Frustration made Utz's head feel like it was bursting at the seams. Disgusted with himself, Utz gave in. It would save him a couple hours of futile arguments. "Fine. Take the spaceship, but I need a ride back to the Onyx Islands. Tomorrow at noon."

Diamond swiveled and stuck out a bony hand.

Reluctantly, Utz shook it.

"Done," they both said together.

Diamond threw back her head and laughed. She pranced to her father and started beating on his shoulders, saying, "Daddy, I'm a ship captain!"

Ancel laughed, too, and said. "It has a nice ring to it, Captain Diamond Fallstar."

A NEW CAPTAIN

The next day, about mid-afternoon, Mitzi rushed into their clearing and cried, "Utz is coming back. He just radioed ahead to say that he'll need help unloading the ship. Can you be at the port in an hour?"

Dr. Mangot was still sick, so Captain Bulmer stayed with her while Blake and Jake walked through the jungle to the heliport. The path was shaded, and they walked slowly. Still, by the time they reached the heliport, Jake was sweating profusely. The planet was getting hotter and hotter.

They found a shady spot and half dozed as they waited. Jake was curious what Utz's urgent business had been. He didn't really care what it was so long as their escape route came back intact.

Finally, the spaceship came in with a roar. Utz was a careful pilot, but this time, the spaceship wobbled and almost missed the pad.

The hatch opened and Utz appeared in the doorway, followed by a skinny red-headed boy. No, a young girl. Her hair was braided in back, and she wore the Fallstar's red. Where had Utz picked her up? And why?

Blake was there first with his hand extended. "I'm Commander Blake Rose of the U.S. Navy."

The girl drew herself up straight. Jake wasn't surprised when she announced, "I am Captain Diamond Fallstar, Captain of the *Tokyo*, and soon to be Admiral of the Bo-See Fleet."

Jake could barely stifle his laugh. She was a Fallstar, all right, so pompous and overly impressed with her own importance. On Earth—if she made it there—she'd be the one to splash photos all over social media. That thought made Jake think of Jillian, his friend who also loved social media. But they weren't alike. Jillian posted photos for fun; Diamond would do it to be noticed.

Suddenly, Jake sobered. Had Diamond said that she was the Captain of the *Tokyo*? He nodded his head at Utz and asked, "What's going on?"

Utz just jerked at a heavy load, pulling it to the gangplank. "A little help here," he grunted.

Jake stepped up and bent to heave the boxes. "What's in here?"

Utz straightened and frowned. "My stuff. I've sold the ship to Diamond."

"What? How will we get out of here?" Jake felt a huge vacuum well up inside, and fear rushed in to fill it. The *Tokyo* was their insurance that they'd escape this doomed planet.

"Your stepfather said he'd be here with a big ship when it was time to evacuate. He'd better come through on that promise because we don't have another option."

Jake sucked in a breath. They were left to the whims of Swann. Any other time, he would've sworn that Swann would come through. But these days were unpredictable. If Swann decided that some orphanage needed to evacuate first, he'd save them and let the Earth scientists die. No, no, he tried to argue with himself. Swann knew the importance of this team to those who would go to Earth. He might sacrifice Jake—after all, he was a Quad-de who would understand—but not the future of the Risonians on Earth.

Too cynical, Jake railed against himself. Swann will be here.

Blake said, "Do you realize that we could die here if the timing is off on anything?"

Utz crossed his arms and glared. "Yes. Everything is risky. But it's my ship and my decision." He nodded to Diamond. "Take off, before I change my mind."

Diamond whistled and skipped back aboard. The ramp retracted.

"Wait!" Jake called.

He tried to reach the ship, but Utz stood in the way. His arms weren't crossed now. Instead, he clenched and unclenched his fists, as if he was a time bomb with a lit fuse.

Jake backed up, arms held up in a gesture of peace.

The spaceship's doors slid closed. A few minutes later, the spaceship lifted off and headed back across the ocean toward Marasca.

Utz turned to glare at the disappearing spaceship.

Jake watched it disappear with a sinking feeling. This tropical island suddenly felt like a prison. He had to call Swann and make sure they had a way off this planet.

But he worried: would Swann make it in time?

A FOLK TALE

The mid-afternoon sun made the beaches glaring hot. Earth's medical team was gathered, as usual, on the shadowed porch, out of the heat.

"What did Swann have to say?" Blake asked.

Minutes ago, Jake had made an emergency radio call to Swann. The equipment was inside the resort's office, so everyone gave him privacy. With so much ash in the air, the sound quality was poor, with lots of static. But he could still make it out. He had explained that Utz no longer had a spaceship, and that they needed a definite evacuation time.

After signing off, he couldn't sit, too upset to settle for even a minute.

He strode back to the porch and announced, "We need to be off-planet in two days. The Brown Matter's pull on the planetary core is increasing exponentially, which means it's drastic changes every day. The planet might hold for a week before it collapses into a black hole, but to be safe, two days."

Dr. Mangot lay on one of the couches, still feverish. Her hair was limp, her clothes rumpled. "No," she moaned. "We have to find the male starfish. We need breeding pairs."

Captain Bulmer sat beside her and said soothingly. "It's OK, Bea. We'll do what we can. We'll dive again at dusk."

He held a glass of water to Dr. Mangot's lips, and she gratefully sipped.

Utz nodded to Jake. "Is he bringing a ship to take us up to Cadee?"

"Yes," he said. "Dawn, day after tomorrow. That gives us about 39 to 40 hours."

Looking around, he saw the same fear on the others' faces that he felt. If they were here when the planet imploded, they'd die.

Dr. Mangot sat up suddenly and called, "Now ye've gone and done it." Her Scottish accent was strong as the fever took her off into outlandish tales. "You've disturbed the Ashrays."

Captain Bulmer said, "Now, Bea, there aren't any such things."

"Water Lover, they call 'em. Ghosts. You can see straight through them."

"Likely someone saw a large jellyfish and thought it was a spirit," Captain Bulmer said soothingly. "That's crazy talk; t'was just a jellyfish."

Her eyes grew large. They were rimmed red with fever, and she was sweating. "You think I'm crazy talking. But I've seen an Ashray."

"When?" Jake asked. Anything to distract him from their situation was welcome. Even a fever-crazed story.

"I was sixteen years old and anxious to be away from Aberforth Hills. Some days, I'd make the long swim to shore, dress and dance at the get-togethers in Coldingham Bay. Ah, what fun that was. One night, I was going back home, early morning, almost dawn, and I saw her."

"Her?" Blake asked. "Ashrays are female?"

Dr. Mangot waved a weak hand, as if swatting at spider webs. "They love the night, you know." From sweating a moment ago, she was now shivering.

Captain Bulmer put a blanket over her shoulders and shrugged at the others. She'd already had her medicines, so there was nothing to do for her, except keep her company and let her rant.

"Anyway," Dr. Mangot went on. "I saw her shimmering in the water. And she spoke to me."

"In English or in Ashray?" Captain Bulmer joked.

Dr. Mangot merely looked at him in pity. "Doesn't matter. I would've understood either one. Anyway, she told me that I was a true daughter of Aberforth Hills, and I should devote myself to her." She stopped. "And since that day—" She took a big gulp of air. "—that city is my true love." Her voice dribbled to a whisper. "Only Aberforth Hills. Will I see her again?" Her voice took on a forlorn air.

Jake thought of the magical city in the North Sea and was instantly nostalgic, too. It was Em's heritage, not his, but he wanted to share it with her. He thought of how fragile Em had looked, pale and tired. Would they ever see Aberforth Hills again? Would he ever see Em again?

Captain Bulmer patted Dr. Mangot's arm. "It's OK, Bea. You'll see her again. Soon. Just sleep and get well."

She turned her back to the rest and seemed calmer after the story. Jake realized they were all tightly wound. Nerves. Dr. Mangot didn't sound any crazier than he felt. Everyone was worried: would they ever see Earth again?

HUNTING STARFISH

Getting ready to dive that night, Jake made sure the nets were in good shape while Blake checked his marine flashlight batteries. They were weak. He'd brought about four dozen extras, but after diving every night for a week, he only had six left, enough to refill his flashlights two more times.

Jake shrugged. "Weak light or not, you'll have to use it until it gives out totally."

"I guess," Blake said uncertainly. "But it's a pain to go topside to change batteries."

"I've got a backup," Jake said. He rummaged in his equipment bag and pulled out his unused marine flashlight. It had been a last-minute addition, and he hadn't even turned it on yet.

"Thanks," Blake said. He hooked it onto his belt pack and turned to check his scuba gear. The compressor had been running all day, refilling the scuba tanks.

Jake hoped this would be their last dive. They desperately needed to find something tonight.

At dusk, they cast off the sailboat, heading away from the brilliant sunset that stained the western sky. There was no wind that evening, so Captain Bulmer had to use some of their scarce fuel to motor outside the bay. There they caught a slight breeze, so he shut down the engine.

In the sudden quiet, Jake heard the cry of a marine bird and looked up. Wings tucked in tight, it dove, striking the water with huge talons, and coming up with something in its mouth.

Majestic.

It was the only word to describe the bird. The bird spread its huge wingspan, floating on the winds. Jake's heart ached, knowing that soon he'd be one of the last people in the universe to ever see such a magnificent sight. Rison held so many wonders that he'd never seen, would never see. The impending tragedy was beyond words.

Two days. Maybe a week. Everything would be gone.

And amidst that heavy grief, they had to focus on one elusive species of starfish. It seemed ironic somehow. Instead, he wanted to embrace everything about Rison and store it up in his heart. But he'd never know even a fraction of a whole planet teeming with life.

That starfish, though, meant life to Em and the Phoke. They had to succeed tonight.

Dr. Mangot leaned against the cabin, dozing. She'd insisted on coming and not being left behind.

"I don't want to be alone when the world ends," she had whispered.

Of course, Captain Bulmer had carried her aboard and made her as comfortable as he could.

Blake hunched over his scuba gear, double checking everything. Utz and Jake sat in the bow, staring at the shadowed islands in front of them. They'd learned that the female *umjaadi* starfish congregated between the first and second islands. Nearby, they would search deep pools where the ocean floor dropped into darkness. If they were going to find the male starfish, it would be in the depths of that inky sea. Or so they hoped.

Finally, Captain Bulmer dropped anchor and everyone except Dr. Mangot dove. Jake let his dive pull him deep and deeper. His catch bag hung at his waist, and he carried a net. But he also had on gloves so he could grab at a starfish if needed and not get stung.

The murky water was like diving through his own desperation.

Unable to see anything, he turned skyward and found Blake who was flashing his light around and moving slowly. Reluctantly, Jake made himself slow down and stay level with Blake. He was methodical and wouldn't go deeper until he was ready. The waters were warm, comforting. Jake could stay down all night, so it was Blake's scuba gear that would limit this search.

Jake guessed they were about sixty feet deep when Blake's flashlight suddenly went dark. A moment later, a stronger light flashed on. Blake was switching to Jake's marine flashlight. But the light was strange. Blake must've accidentally put it on ultraviolet or UV mode. He shone the light into the depths, and suddenly Jake saw three blue streaks of light flashing at him.

The UV light was reflecting from a fish! Why hadn't they thought of this? On Earth, scientists often used ultraviolet light to show things not visible with the naked eye. What else would they see?

Jake excitedly wrote on his slate: UV!

Blake nodded and pointed downward. Quickly, they kicked deeper.

There. A wheel made of five green lights. Was it an octopus-like creature or—a starfish? Excited, Jake dashed forward, and with gloved hands, he grabbed the creature and shoved it into his catch bag. It was likely a starfish, but in the dark, he couldn't tell if it was what they needed. They'd have to go topside to figure it out.

Then, below him, he felt a rush of hot water, and a red glow suddenly appeared. A new magma vent had exploded beneath them, creating an opening for magma to flow. As predicted, the planet's mantle was cracking.

Jake turned and grabbed Blake's arm and pointed upward. The magma would heat the water quickly here. But Blake pointed to his watch: he had to decompress.

Jake's heart squeezed, nervous about how big the vent would get and how fast. They couldn't rush the decompression; he'd learned that on Earth when he dove with a variety of naval officers from around the world. Captain Meryl Puentes developed Decompression Sickness, and the last he'd heard, was still unable to walk.

Quickly, Blake kicked upward to his next decompression level and stopped. He set his timer, and they waited.

And waited.

The red smear below them spread, magma pouring into the ocean below. Through his gills, Jake smelled sulfur. Desperately, he tried to think of other things, to speed up the time, to get Dad to safety. But they had to wait.

And wait.

And wait.

Finally, Blake's alarm vibrated, and they could move upward to the next level. Below, the red haze had spread to cover half of Jake's vision. However, it seemed to have slowed. Or maybe Jake's sense of time was distorted. What if it suddenly broke through with a huge column of magma? Without think-ing, Jake pulled his feet up and hugged his knees.

Silly! he thought. *Getting my toes two feet higher isn't going to matter.* Yet somehow, it felt marginally safer.

In the dark, it was impossible to see if Blake was anxious or calm. He waited, and that's all Jake knew. No sense in using flashlight batteries just to watch each other trying to control a panic. The others were already top side, and Captain Bulmer would have the anchor up and sails ready to go when they arrived.

Finally, Blake's watch vibrated. Briefly, he flashed the light down toward the rising magma.

Blake's face glowed eerily in the UV light. Behind his mask, Blake's eyes were wide with a barely controlled panic.

Hurry, Jake wanted to scream. *We need to get out!*

Jake glanced down at the magma again. There, just below them were dozens of flashing lights, reflections from Blake's UV light. Jake recognized the green wheel that meant the tips of a starfish were lit up. He wanted to dash down, grab several and dash back up. But Blake was already kicking upward as fast as he could.

Jake shook his catch bag. He still had one starfish and he wasn't even sure it was an *umjaadi*, much less a male *umjaadi*. Reluctantly, he turned away from the starfish who were rising in a vain attempt to escape the spreading magma. They might not get away, but Jake could. He *mokwa* his legs and surged upward. From behind, he shoved Blake while Captain Bulmer tugged from above. Blake clambered awkwardly over the ship's hull and fell onto the decking.

Jake quickly climbed the ladder, and Captain Bulmer sprinted back to the bow to release the sails and handle the rudder. Fortunately, the breeze had picked up, and the sails caught the wind. Briskly, Captain Bulmer sailed away, keep-ing the sails as taut as possible.

At the dock, they all tumbled out, anxious to get to the highest ground possible.

Captain Bulmer tied up the sail boat and half carried Dr. Mangot up the cliff. Almost shaking with relief, Jake helped Blake take off his scuba gear. They both grabbed tanks and trotted up toward the resort. Halfway up, though, Blake had to stop and catch his breath.

Jake stopped with him. He turned to stare back at the spot they'd left. Was it his imagination or was steam rising from that area?

They turned and toiled up the slope, the scuba tanks banging at Jake's legs. When they reached the top, he suddenly remembered his catch bag. He dropped the tanks with a thud and grabbed at the net bag. The strings caught. Quickly, he tugged and it unknotted, dropping the starfish into his hands.

"Look!" he called. The others came from the resort's porch to see what he had. "It's an *umjaadi* male!"

They crowded around and talked excitedly. They could leave and get off planet. A couple males would be better, but with one, they could go. But their elation fell away when they realized it was dead. It had been out of water too long.

Jake cursed himself for not going back down and grabbing a dozen of them. Cursed himself for not checking the bag earlier and hanging it off the boat's side where it would dangle in the water. Or grabbing a bucket of sea water to dunk it in.

Now, they had to make at least one more dive. They had an easy means to find the male *umjaadi* by using the UV flashlight—if the batteries lasted. But the new vent had ruined that spot and probably killed off all the starfish. Only one day left to find what they needed to heal Em. He held his head and rocked. Only 24 hours before Swann would arrive with a space ship to evacuate them. They had to find another group of male starfish.

ULTRAVIOLET

Everyone agreed that they'd dive again in the morning after a couple hours' rest. With the UV lights, they hoped it wouldn't matter what time of day they went.

Even the dawn air shimmered with heat. Heavy smog from the volcanic eruptions worldwide had finally reached their remote location. Or maybe new volcanos had erupted in the ocean and were now tall enough to spew ash into the air. Either way, Jake struggled to breathe.

"Find a kerchief or cloth to tie over your face. If it gets worse a wet cloth is even better," Dr. Mangot suggested. She was sitting up drinking a cup of herbal tea. Her face was calmer and her voice stronger.

She's still weak, Jake thought. But she might be over the worst of the illness. Em relapsed easily, though, so she should take it easy.

After some convincing from Captain Bulmer, she'd decided that a day sitting in the shade of the porch would be good for her. With a calmer mind, she didn't panic about being left alone.

From across the yard, Jake heard the air compressors switch off. He stopped by his room and tore one of his oldest shirts into strips. He tied one over his nose and mouth and went to help Blake with his scuba tanks.

When they gathered by the top of the beach path, Jake passed out the other strips to Captain Bulmer and Utz, and they gratefully tied them in place. At the dock, they clambered onto the sail boat and cast off. The air was so still that Captain Bulmer had to start the motor. They had no extra fuel cans on board. They couldn't go far. Fortunately, once they were out of the bay, they picked up wind, and Captain Bulmer switched off the engine.

Meanwhile, Utz and Jake had been studying a map of the islands.

"We've got to try farther out," Utz said.

Jake nodded and finally pointed to a nameless island to the east. The depth charts showed water at least as deep as where they dove yesterday. Maybe they'd get lucky. Utz nodded his agreement.

Holding the cloth over his nose and mouth, Jake showed the map to Captain Bulmer. He nodded agreement, too, and changed course, heading directly east.

The water was choppy, splashing over the boat's bow.

Captain Bulmer called, "We're in more open seas here. Sure you want to go this way?"

Utz shrugged. "It's about the only option."

The boat was silent, everyone lost in his own thoughts. As the far island neared, Blake shrugged on his wet suit and zipped it up. By the time Captain Bulmer threw out an anchor, Blake was ready. He fell backwards off the side of the boat and disappeared into the dark waters.

Jake shrugged and dove in after him. He zipped his legs together and kicked downward toward Blake's flashlight. The water was murkier than ever, a sign that the underwater magma flows were polluting the water. Jake realized that he was holding his arms out from his body so his gills would get more water flow. It was hard to breathe. He kicked harder and tapped Blake's shoulder.

Jake reached for Blake's slate that hung from his waist belt. He wrote: "Can't breathe. Must go up."

Blake's eyes widened. He nodded.

"You come up, too!" Jake wrote.

Blake shook his head. "Need that starfish."

"Alone?" Jake wrote.

Blake wrote back. "I'm fine."

Reluctantly, Jake nodded. He kicked upward, feeling faint now, struggling to breathe. With relief, he popped his head above the water and gulped air. Captain Bulmer and Utz sat on the side of the boat about to jump in.

"You OK?" Utz asked.

Jake breathed deeply again, glad that he could breathe in air or water. "No. Water's too polluted. Can't breathe. Blake says he's OK with his scuba gear, so he's looking alone."

"I'll go," Captain Bulmer said. "I don't actually breathe underwater. I just hold my breath for about thirty minutes."

"Thanks," Jake said. "I didn't want him down there alone."

With a nod, Captain Bulmer dove into the water.

Utz helped Jake pull out onto the sail boat's deck.

"Ironic," Utz said. "The Earthlings can swim our seas, and we can't."

It should've been easy, Jake raged to himself. They knew the type of waters where the male starfish lived. They had the UV lights to make them visible. Captain Bulmer, Utz and Jake should've been able to stay underwater for as long as it took to find the male starfish.

But the waters of Rison—at least here in the Jewel Islands—were now poisoned for Risonians. If the ash and magma had poisoned the waters here, it was probably wide-spread. He could only imagine the panic in the underwater cities. They'd have to evacuate to land. But would they? They were going to die soon, no matter what they did. The deep sorrow rose again, threatening to overwhelm him.

I can't think about that, Jake told himself. He only had energy to think about getting the starfish that might cure Em. Later, there would be time to mourn.

INTO THE DEPTHS

Blake carefully controlled his breathing, setting up a slow, regular rhythm that would conserve the air in his tanks. His light didn't penetrate far in the murk. He hovered and switched to UV light. Someone tapped his shoulder.

Blake spun around and nodded when he recognized Captain Bulmer.

Captain Bulmer wrote on his slate: I can only stay down about 30 minutes. We need to search fast.

Blake nodded and flashed his UV light in an arc. Nothing.

They kicked along together, watching the sweep of UV light, hoping for the six-legged star. Nothing.

Perhaps the pollution had killed them all and they'd never find a male.

Suddenly, there was a flash of something, off to Blake's right side. Sweeping the UV light, Blake turned. Before him was a dark mass with tentacles that lit up. Not a starfish, Blake realized. Whatever it was, it was massive.

Blake switched the light off, plunging them into darkness. He dared not turn it on again.

I'm not scared, he told himself. Just cautious of the unknown.

Captain Bulmer and Blake hung suspended, not moving, for several minutes before Captain Bulmer tapped Blake's hand in a signal to try the light again.

The creature had moved on. But they had to be careful, or the UV light would attract other marine life. They wanted to attract the right marine life, the *umjaadi* male starfish. Blake shrugged. They had to risk it. He just wished he had a good Earth-made harpoon as protection. When they'd swum with Utz and Jake, he hadn't worried because this was their ocean and they'd know when to worry. Without the Risonians, the unknown loomed larger.

Still, Blake had always pursued the unknown. He'd always wanted to find that next species to study. Just not now. Not when they only had 24 hours at the most to find the *umjaadi* and get out of here.

They were circumnavigating the tiny island, and on the northern side, they ran into a patch of seaweed that grew upwards, reaching for the skies overhead. It was shallower here, so normally, they'd get some filtered light. Instead, Blake had to keep his flashlight on, using up even more battery power. The *umjaadi* wouldn't be in this shallow area, so they quickly swam on. The currents were rougher on the west side because the currents flowed west to east here. That meant it wasn't protected enough for the *umjaadi's* habitat.

Blake began to despair, but they had no choice but to keep swimming. As they rounded the southern end of the island, Captain Bulmer stopped.

He pulled out his slate: Do you feel colder water?

Blake shrugged and plucked at his wetsuit.

Deeper, Captain Bulmer wrote. Let me get some air and we'll dive.

Blake nodded and waited for Captain Bulmer to surface and breathe deeply for a few minutes. Then, together they dove. The land dropped precipitously here, making Blake feel like he was hang-gliding from atop a huge cliff. They kicked harder, going deeper. Blake switched the light to UV again.

In the dark water, the UV light didn't penetrate far, maybe just 10 feet. At the edge of their vision something danced.

Another huge creature?

No. This time, it was a school of tiny fish that darted toward them. Their heads glowed but their tails were dark, making them look like tiny glowing globes. Blake felt the familiar longing, the passion to know everything there was to know about this new species. But the globe-headed fish darted in and around them, and then disappeared.

Blake told himself: *Concentrate. Time is short.*

They kicked even deeper. Blake glanced at his wrist depth indicator. If he went much deeper, he'd have to spend a long time decompressing. He stopped and wrote on his slate: Can you scout deeper? DCS worry.

He hated to stop just because of the DCS problem. It felt like he was weak, helpless. Human. In the oceans, here or on Earth, humans were weak: at risk for death from the weight of the water, lack of oxygen, or poisonous and predatory animals. Captain Bulmer was a strong Phoke, at home in the water, even with all its dangers.

Captain Bulmer nodded and took Blake's flashlight. He kicked hard. He wouldn't have much time left before he had to go up to breathe.

Blake watched the light going deeper and deeper.

Deeper and deeper, smaller and smaller.

Until Blake lost sight of Captain Bulmer in the depths.

THE SICK PLANET

Utz and Jake hung over the rail of the boat, watching for signs of the swimmers. Time dragged by.

Jake worried: *Where are you, Dad?*

He still called him Dad in his mind, even though he always called him Blake out loud. Dad was always going off in search of some new species. So far, he had four species of animals named after him: one bird, one fish, one insect and one butterfly. Dad didn't care what animal group—amphibians, mammals, birds, fish, or insects. He just wanted to study a new species, to compare it with all known species and classify it. *Kind of nerdy*, Jake thought. *But kind of interesting at the same time.*

It's why Mom and Dad met in the first place.

Utz growled, "This air is foul. We need to get off-planet soon."

Jake nodded grimly.

"When we're on Earth," Utz said, "Will we be quarantined in the same place?"

"I think so, but details are sketchy. Mom says there will be a remote desert location for all Risonians."

"Except her." Utz looked up at the angry red blur of the sun. "She'll be free to travel."

Jake shook his head, "I don't think so. She'll have to join us in the desert."

"It won't work, you know. Too many smugglers," Utz said.

"Like Captain Diamond?" Jake said, struggling to keep the tinge of anger from his voice. He still didn't understand why Utz had traded away their backup escape vehicle.

"Smugglers have been sneaking Risonians into Earth for years, and no one has noticed. Of course, they didn't break an *umjaadi* globe and spill everything into Earth's oceans."

Jake was glad for the discussion because it was a distraction. He sat on the boat's edge and let his legs dangle over. The air was still smoggy, and the cloth filter over his mouth and nose was hot and uncomfortable. "How many Risonians are on Earth by now?"

Utz shrugged. "A thousand. Maybe two. Could be two or three times that for all I know. My cousin, Ancel Fallstar, doesn't exactly share information with me."

"What?" The official count was about 25 Risonians, all in his mother's ambassadorial office. A couple thousand other Risonian scattered around the world was amazing. And that didn't count the secret installations like Seastead. "How long has Fallstar been smuggling in people?"

"About fifteen years. At first, he only had one ship, and it was hard to avoid Earth's detection. But he learned. And then, he bribed. There've been regular shipments to and from Earth for at least five years." Utz leaned against the mast and re-laxed. "Might as well tell you now because it'll be pointless in a day or two. And you should know that there are wealthy Risonians on Earth. Lots of money has been funneled to them."

Jake nodded slowly. Wealthy. Yes, any smugglers moving to Earth would be wealthy because they were, well, smug-glers. They didn't care about laws or rules. They just cared about making money. Well, most that he'd met cared about their families, too. Just not about laws or rules.

And those that they smuggled would be from important families, rich enough to pay. They'd set up bank accounts and find some way for funds from Rison to trickle into them. After all, families on Rison wouldn't need the money. Suddenly, Jake wondered if that's what Swann had been doing all along. Was he sending money to Dayexi, building up a cushion of funds for them to live on when he got there?

Without warning, the planet shivered, as if it was sick and running a temperature and knew that unless something drastic happened soon, it would meet its destiny.

On land, Jake might have sat down or run for high ground. In a sailboat, they just had to wait it out. Waves sloshed around their boat, and it strained against its anchor. But gradually, the waters calmed again.

Jake peered into the water, now an angry green, and groaned. *Where are you, Dad?*

Sooner, rather than later, they had to get off planet.

ULTRAVIOLET

Blake blinked, not sure of what he was seeing. A small glow had reappeared and he had assumed Captain Bulmer was coming back up. But the light was wrong. It appeared to dangle and swing about aimlessly. But Blake dared not go down to investigate or help. He couldn't risk the DCS.

Another Risonian would've been helpful, he thought with frustration.

As Captain Bulmer rose, Blake caught flashes of something glowing in the UV lights. But everything was so shaky, he couldn't be sure. An irrational hope grew in him, though. Maybe they'd found the starfish and they could leave this cursed planet.

Captain Bulmer was close enough now to see that he carried something in his hands. When he was ten feet away, Blake darted down and caught at the UV light, unsnapping it from Captain Bulmer's waist belt.

He shone it directly on the Phoke. He gasped, making his mouthpiece fall out of his mouth. Fumbling with the mouthpiece, he found it hard to replace in his mouth because of his grin. Captain Bulmer held six large starfish. The UV light revealed their six legs, and they all looked healthy.

Motioning, Blake asked if he should carry some. Captain Bulmer shook his head, but nodded upwards. He needed to breathe!

Blake was double-glad now that he hadn't ventured so deep that he had to decompress. They kicked briskly, surfacing a moment later. Captain Bulmer gasped, letting himself relax in the air.

Abruptly, the planet shook again.

It was disorienting in the water. Captain Bulmer was still struggling to get his breath, and suddenly waves crashed over him. It lasted only five or ten seconds—or a lifetime. When it ended, Captain Bulmer gasped and called, "I've dropped them! Help!"

Immediately, Blake replaced his mouthpiece and dove having enough sense to shine the UV light ahead of him. He kicked hard, his flippers making his legs ache. Flashing in the

UV lights, the starfish pirouetted, a weirdly beautiful ballet as they fell back toward their home in the depths.

Blake kicked even harder, but they fell away faster than ever. Frustration gave him a last burst of energy and he reached for a spinning sestet of lights. There, he had the starfish. At least they had one.

But suddenly, he held only a leg and the starfish was gone. He'd pulled off the leg, or the starfish's defense mechanisms allowed it to lose a leg rather than lose its life.

Helpless, Blake watched the starfish dancing toward home. They had lost them all.

WAITING

They returned to the dock exhausted and beaten. They'd missed the male starfish, and all they had was one preserved dead one, and the leg of another.

Dr. Mangot insisted that they seal the leg in a glow globe on the outside chance that it would regrow from just the leg. Not likely, but it was all they had. Dr. Mangot moaned that if she could think straight, there might be something she could add to the water to encourage regeneration of the missing parts.

Anyway, it no longer mattered. The Earth delegation had to get off-planet before it was too late.

The ground was rumbling now, the planet's core humming and thrumming, singing to itself. It warbled and burbled, magma coming closer to the surface than ever. Jake couldn't escape the sound, and it grated at his nerves. Already taut with worry, he felt like he would break at any moment.

By evening, dead fish washed ashore all along the beaches, making small piles where the waves dropped them. In another day, the stench would be—

Another day! What a foolish thought, Jake chided himself.

Captain Bulmer urged them to pack and sleep near the heliport.

Jake quickly threw things into his bags, taking only what he needed for the journey back to Earth. He gazed a long time at the photo he'd taken from Swann's office. It showed Swann hugging him while Mom smiled. He opened the frame and pulled out the photo. He stuffed it in his shirt. Everything else, he left in his bedroom. To speed things up, he went to help Blake with his packing.

Blake stood staring at the air compressors, scuba tanks, and other gear. He waved at the pile and murmured, "Guess I don't need those."

Jake looked up sharply. Blake sounded drunk or—sick? His face was flushed red.

"Dad, sit." He gently pushed Blake to a chair.

"You called me Dad." When he looked up at Jake, Blake's eyes were red.

Almost in a panic, Jake raced to Dr. Mangot's room and banged on the door.

"Come in."

Shoving open the door, Jake saw Captain Bulmer hovering over Dr. Mangot. She was flushed again, but standing. Wobbling. She took a tentative step, and her knees collapsed. Captain Bulmer caught her smoothly.

He led her back to sit on the bed. Feeling behind her, Dr. Mangot swiveled and lay down.

Captain Bulmer turned to Jake. "What?"

"I think Blake's sick now. I need a thermometer."

Captain Bulmer swore. He grabbed a thermometer from the bedside table and handed it to Jake. Then he paused, rummaged in a small bag, and pulled out a bottle of pills. "Antibiotics. Follow the directions. And then, we've got to get them moved to the helipad, sick or not."

It was a grim few hours. They decided to take Dr. Mangot first and come back for Blake. They all wore cloths over their noses and mouths, but still the foul air made everything harder. They took turns carrying Dr. Mangot, and at the last, supported her between them. Utz went along, loaded down with half of their bags. Reluctantly, they left her alone at the helipad.

When they'd arrived, the jungle was a blur to Jake. After a week on the island, though, the jumble had turned into tall palm-like trees, huge ferns and lots of undergrowth. They found a soft spot for Dr. Mangot under a fern and went back for Blake, repeating the process, while Utz lugged the last of their bags. All the glow stars with starfish were in one box, rather large and unwieldy.

The two trips left Jake exhausted. Briefly, he radioed Swann, who assured him through the increasing static that they'd be there at dawn. He drank, ate and dozed.

A tremor woke him, the planet groaning and grumbling beneath them. Checking the time, he saw that it was two hours past midnight. Quickly, he checked on Blake, whose temperature was still high. He shook out another antibiotic and made Blake swallow it. Blake probably wouldn't remember taking it in the morning because he instantly sank back into sleep.

Jake wished he could see the stars. Instead, the smoke clouds hid the constellations, making the night inky black. Soon, very soon, they needed to be among the stars. He paced carefully, where he knew the ground was clear, counting precise steps, five one way and five to return.

He checked his radio again to be sure the batteries were charged, and it was turned on. He wanted to call Swann, but that was pointless. He would be here as fast as he could.

The hours dragged by. Jake knew he should sit and try to sleep, but instead he paced. Every rumble made him jump. Every slight tremor made him freeze. Nerves on edge, he felt his fears mount as the sky lightened. There was no dawn in the smog, but rather a lightening of the sky into a dim shroud over the land.

Finally, there was a radio call, crackly and broken up, but definitely Swann's voice. "Norio and I will be there in an hour. Be ready. The planet isn't going to last long."

Jake woke Utz and Captain Bulmer. They woke Dr. Mangot and Blake long enough to dose them, make them go to the bathroom, and make them drink something. After those wearying tasks, the two patients sank back into uneasy sleep.

EVACUATION

Jake stared at his chronometer, still set to Earth time. January 23. They'd been on the planet for eight days. Would this day live in infamy as the day Rison imploded? Or did they have three or four more days as the scientists had predicted?

The radio crackled again. 'Navi—. . . have to. . .ready.'

The volcanic ash in the atmosphere had nearly blocked communications.

Jake waved at the others. "Get ready. They're close."

The ground trembled without stopping now, as if the planet was shuddering in horror.

Suddenly, lights shone out of the dark sky, and ashen wind blasted down on them.

The small band crouched to diminish the effect of the down drafts from the spaceship.

After the spaceship landed, the door popped open, and a gangplank extended. Swann and Norio strode down the gangplank calling, "Let's go. Now!"

Captain Bulmer staggered forward, Dr. Mangot in his arms.

Jake shook Blake, who woke with a lazy smile. Blake yawned, stretched, and drawled, "Wow, I feel better. That medicine must've helped."

"Good," Jake said. "Because we've got to evacuate."

Jake helped Blake stand. After momentary dizziness, Blake held up his hands and said, "I got this."

He trudged toward the gangplank, not exactly racing, but steady on his feet and not wobbling. Jake was encouraged. They were almost off this doomed planet.

They followed Utz who carried several bags.

Norio took the bags from him and said quietly. "No extra weight."

"We'll need the starfish box at least," Utz said.

Norio nodded and Utz went to carry it aboard.

Swann stopped Blake at the bottom of the gangplank. "We need to talk."

Jake hung back long enough to hear their first words.

"Back in Killia, it was a mad scramble to take off. I had to give up our larger ship, so this is the only one we had left." Swann shrugged, as if that statement should tell Blake something.

Norio added, "We used the *Eagle 10* to evacuate the household personnel. But we misjudged the time. We thought there was time for another trip up and down before we'd need it for this trip. As it was, we barely got it off before we came here for you."

His eyes met Jake's. The household was safe, and that had been Norio's main concern. Jake nodded his understanding.

Blake turned to stare at the spaceship. For a moment, there was nothing, and then Blake's face screwed up in some awful emotion. Hoarsely, he whispered, "It's too small for seven people."

Swann gave a small nod.

Jake felt a horror grow in him. It was a tiny ship, no bigger than the *Tokyo*. A four-seater. From the sound of it, this one had a standard engine. At least the *Tokyo*'s engine had been enhanced for speed and power.

He glared at his stepfather and mentally recounted their small group. There wasn't room for all of them. Swann and Norio obviously had to go. Likewise, Captain Bulmer and Dr. Mangot had to go, or Earth would roar with outrage. That left zero spots for Jake, Utz and Blake.

If they were very lucky, the ship might take a fifth passenger. No way would all seven of them make it to the Cadee Moon Base.

Two people had to stay behind.

Why had Swann brought such a small vessel? Jake fumed. But of course, he knew the answer instantly. Swann was, to the end, compassionate to his people. To a fault. Swann had given the larger spaceship, the *Eagle 10*, to his household servants. Like Norio, he would make sure his people were safe, even if it meant difficulties later.

As if they were one, Blake and Swann stepped off the gangplank, far enough away that Jake couldn't hear them talking. He started back down, but Norio reached out and grabbed his arm, pulling him onto the spaceship.

"They'll settle things, and we'll leave. Come on and get strapped in." Norio stepped forward to the pilot's seat and started flipping switches, readying to leave.

Captain Bulmer had already buckled Dr. Mangot into a seat and took the one next to her. Utz staggered aboard with the starfish globes, and Norio helped him strap down the box.

Jake trailed back to the doorway to watch his fathers.

"No!" Blake yelled. "Dayexi needs YOU, not me. Your people need you."

Jake sucked in a breath sharply. They were arguing over who would go and who would stay.

Jake raced down the gangplank, his heart torn. Surely, they could all board, and they'd make it. Surely, no one had to stay.

Blake was still yelling, "With Rison about to implode, the fate of Risonians is now tied to that of Earthlings. Irrevocably. They will need your diplomacy."

"No," Swann said firmly. He looked over Blake's head and waved at Jake. "Go back onboard!"

Jake screamed, "No!"

His voice hit Blake like a physical blow, and he staggered back, and then turned to stare at Jake. Blake's face was pale and sober in the murk. He already looked like a ghost.

"No!" Jake screamed again, and he didn't know if he was crying for his stepfather or his biological father. Both men had to make it off the planet. He loved them both.

Blake looked back toward Swann, and his head jerked backward. Swann had punched him in the nose. Blood spurted out, and Blake bent double to howl. Swann brought a knee up and again Blake's head jerked. He fell backward, spread-eagled. He tried to sit, shaking his head.

Swann grabbed Blake under his armpits and dragged him up the gangplank, his shoes bumping. Norio was there to shove Jake back into the ship, and then to help Swann with Blake's struggling form. As soon as Blake was inside the ship, Swann sprang back and yelled, "Go!"

Instead, without Swann holding him, Blake managed to kick away from Norio and charged out of the spaceship, down the gangplank and tackled Swann.

Captain Bulmer, Utz and Dr. Mangot were frozen, undecided what to do in this foolish, deadly struggle.

Jake watched from the doorway, his heart in his mouth. Norio started down the gangplank again to help. But Jake grabbed at his shirt and jerked. "No. You can't interfere."

Norio shook him off. Tears streamed down Norio's cheeks, and his voice was hoarse. "The Prime Minister has given me an order. And I'll die trying to obey it."

Jake understood. If Swann was determined to stay here on Rison as it imploded, then Norio could only honor that choice. He had to do as Swann had asked, or die trying. Otherwise, there was no honor left to him, no way to show a lifetime of respect for the man who was his boss, his friend, his mentor.

But Jake had to stop Norio from helping Swann sacrifice himself.

Suddenly, Captain Bulmer was there, huge and bulking. He grabbed Norio in a bear hug. Utz clambered into the pilot's seat and readied the spaceship for lift-off. Norio stopped struggling and watched Utz instead of the fight. After a minute, he nodded and turned back to the struggle.

Outside the ship, Swann and Blake were exchanging blows, fighting for the honor of sacrificing himself for the people of Rison, for Dayexi, and for Jake.

Without warning, a massive quake shook everything. For seven seconds, the world heaved and bucked. When it stopped, the air was still, as if everything was holding its breath.

Then a strange creaking started. Looking around, Jake saw one of the tallest palm trees swaying. Slowly, it toppled.

It landed on the gangplank with a tremendous boom.

The ship was stuck fast and couldn't lift off!

Captain Bulmer, Jake, Swann and Blake hurried to heave at the tree's trunk. Heavy, it was still half-stuck to the ground by roots, so it wouldn't move.

Norio pulled an axe from an equipment cabinet and ran to the roots. Captain Bulmer took the axe and shoved Norio out of the way. The Captain's bulk made the axe's head bite faster and deeper.

Still, the others shoved at the tree trunk.

Swann grunted and said, "Blake, you've got to see the sense in this. I'm Risonian. I'd be lost on Earth."

"Dayexi has found a way to be happy there," Blake said evenly. "You will, too."

"She's found a way to be happy because you've been there to help. She needs you."

Angry, Jake interrupted, "She—we—need both of you."

Swann stopped shoving and put a hand on Jake's shoulder. "Son. You know this is right. You're a true Quad-de, and we don't avoid the truth."

"No. No. No," Jake's voice trembled. Was it because Swann had called him "son"? Because Swann had said he was a true Quad-de? He'd worked hard to make Swann proud of him. Worked to be first on the fight floor. Worked to become a diplomat. Worked to adapt to the moon base and to an Earth school. For Swann.

They stared at each other for a long moment, and then Swann dropped his grip on the tree trunk. He took a step forward and pulled Jake into a hug. His face buried in Swann's chest, Jake breathed deeply of the hint of seaweed, the sweetness of *wolkev*, the smell of home. No. Swann couldn't stay here.

Swann murmured into Jake's ear, "My son."

And Jake wept.

For long heartbeats they stayed like that, father hugging his son and son hugging his father.

A cheer brought them back, and Jake realized that the tree was free from the roots.

Swann turned Jake loose and swiveled toward Blake. Before the Earthling could turn around, Swann locked his hands and brought them down hard on Blake's head.

Blake slumped and slid to the ground.

Utz was already in the pilot's seat, and the gangplank was retracting. Captain Bulmer and Norio ran up the moving gangplank and into the ship. Norio reached down and pulled Jake up and into the spaceship. Swann heaved Blake onto his shoulders. Norio reached down to pull Blake inside, too. But the heavy deadweight was too much for Norio to lift alone. Captain Bulmer leaned over and grabbed a fistful of Blake's shirt and heaved.

At the last moment, just as the door began to close, Norio sat on the edge of the doorway.

No! Jake grabbed for him.

But Norio had already let himself fall to the ground.

No! Jake spoke the word, but nothing came out.

The spaceship lifted off, and its doors closed shut.

Jake scrambled to a window and pressed his face against it.

Swann and Norio stood shoulder to shoulder in the clearing.

Swann lifted one hand in farewell.

His heart full of sorrow, Jake pressed his hand into the glass and watched as they disappeared. Two of the most important men in his life, Risonians through and through, even to the end.

IMPLOSION

As they lifted off and into the planet's outer atmosphere, the spaceship struggled with the weight of five people. Escaping the planet's gravitational pull was hard, making the engine whine.

Jake felt himself pulling in his stomach muscles, as if that would make him lighter and relieve the ship's load. He sat cramped into a small space on the floor between the seats and the box that held the starfish globes. Without his weight, he fretted, the small spaceship would still have struggled, but not as bad.

"Oh!" cried Utz. "No!"

Jake stood and craned to see out the window.

They were already halfway to the moon. Far below them, the planet was a perfect blue ball.

No, not perfect.

A red crack was splitting off the top third of the ball. Agonizingly slow, the crack widened, and it looked like an angry slash, a wound that needed stitches. Impossibly, it widened more, magma pouring out like blood.

It kept widening: the planet was bleeding to death.

Cringing, Jake's hands pressed onto the window glass; he wished he could grab hold of the jagged edges and force the crack to close. If only he could stop it from expanding more.

Another crack appeared at almost a ninety-degree angle from the first. The perfect sphere bulged, lopsided as pressure released at the point of the cracks. Jake's hand involuntarily went to his temple, remembering the times he'd fallen and cracked his head, leaving a huge knot. It was a planetary concussion.

Up till now, only the top third of the planet was involved. Now, like a balloon, the whole globe inflated slightly, pulsing outward. Jake couldn't imagine the force necessary to make an entire planet look like it was inflating.

The planet fell inward.

It was probably rapid, probably over in mere seconds. But to those watching, time slowed.

The dusky blue ocean—they were looking at the Holla Sea—dimpled like an apple where the stem attached. The indentation spun, sucking water, down and down. It must have hit the core's magma because a plume of steam spat toward the sky.

"Look!" cried Utz.

Another cyclone appeared in the North Seas. And then, another in the southern polar region. In massive lazy swirls, water spun toward the center of each funnel and disappeared.

Plumes of steam spread rapidly becoming a dense fog that slowly, slowly, slowly enveloped the whole planet. There were outlines of continents, and then there was white. There was blue water, and then there was white. The blue planet had turned into a cloud of steam.

It was impossible to see what was happening.

And then, even the clouds dimpled and pulled inward, rushing down toward a huge gravity pit, the black hole that was forming at the center of the planet.

Jake thought of the people: a mother nursing her baby, a couple picnicking, someone chopping vegetables for stew, Mitzi building a sand castle, Hideaki fishing for a *mundy*, Swann and Norio—

He wept.

Boom!

A shock wave hit their ship and threw them toward Cadee, the lonely moon that held a tiny remnant of Risonians.

The shock wave jostled Jake, and he lost his footing, grabbing at something to keep from falling into Blake, who was still knocked out and strapped to a chair. He finally caught hold of the base of Dr. Mangot's chair and hung there, frantic to know what was happening.

Utz's face was a stern mask of concentration as he fought to ride the shock wave and fought to keep them on course for Cadee.

Another shock wave hit. Jake curled himself around the chair's base and hid his face. He lay there, frozen in shock and grief. Rison was gone. Swann was gone. What would he and his mother do without Swann?

Another shock wave. And another.

Finally, Utz called out. "We'll dock in five minutes."

GONE

The crowded hallways of the Cadee Moon Base were somber and quiet. Shock. Grief. Sorrow. The words were inadequate for the devastation they had just witnessed.

Gone. All gone.

Everyone lost a loved one. Everyone.

A moment of silence for the lost planet. A lifetime of silence for the lost souls.

They grieved. For the lost beaches, mountain passes, soaring birds and humble beasts. For lost aunts, uncles, cousins, grandparents, husbands, wives, children. For the loss of an entire diverse, exciting planet.

Unspeakable sadness.

The images from Cadee were broadcast to Earth, and Dayexi called, desperate for news.

Blake and Jake faced her together.

"We tried to save Swann," Blake said. "But he knocked me out and shoved me aboard."

Jake could only shake his head and whisper, "He's gone."

Her wails split their already fractured hearts into more splinters. Sharp pain overwhelmed them, and they clung to each other until Dayexi's tears subsided. Finally, she held up a hand to the screen and pleaded, "Come home. Soon."

"Soon," promised Blake. "Soon."

THE CADEE MOON BASE

No one had the luxury of grieving; there was work to do.

Engineers, physicists, aeronautics experts and every other person with technical expertise was drawn into the huge job of stabilizing Cadee Moon as a new satellite around their sun, Turco. They had wisely placed thrusters all around the moon, so they could maneuver as needed. The shock waves had thrown them away from the planet, and they had to avoid the belt of debris left from the planet's destruction.

The plan, many years in the making, of how to place the moon into a stable orbit was tricky and long. It took a blessed concentration that kept people from thinking or feeling.

Meanwhile, people loaded onto ships, saying good-bye to their solar system and blasted off for Earth. Those left behind, waited.

Numb. Empty. Drifting the hallways of the Cadee Moon Base as if they were ghosts.

The Earth delegation expected to blast off almost immediately. Instead, Dr. Mangot went straight to the infirmary where intravenous fluids finally stabilized her temperature. Captain Bulmer hardly left her side until her temperature was normal. Only then did he find a place to sleep for a while.

When Jake realized they'd be delayed, he insisted that someone else take their spaceship, the *Eagle 10*, and they could join a later ship. He traipsed the hallways until he found a small, dingy room filled with people, and waved to the small girl who'd swum with them when they first arrived on Cadee.

He motioned to her father and gestured toward the door. "Mr. Bruce, please."

Mr. Bruce asked cautiously, "Yes? What can I do for you?"

"Let's talk in private," Jake said. They stepped outside into the corridor, and Jake explained their situation. "You can take our ship if you can find a pilot."

Mr. Bruce's eyes rimmed with tears, and he shook Jake's hand. "We're so sorry about Swann Quad-de."

Jake had to turn his head away, or his own tears would spill over.

Mr. Bruce stepped forward and said, "Thank you, sir. You're the head of the Quad-de family now, and we know you'll make us proud on Earth."

Head of the Quad-de family. Jake vowed to himself, "I'll live up to your legacy, Swann."

When the Bruce family loaded onto the spaceship and was about to blast off, Jake stopped by briefly to say good-bye.

Immediately, Merry took his hand and tugged at it.

Looking down, Jake tried to smile. She was the future of the Risonian people. "Do you need something?"

She nodded.

"What do you need?" he asked.

She tugged him lower. Jake sank to his knee and looked at the child. Her curly hair spilled over her eyes, and he brushed it back gently. It made him really look at her.

"What can I do to help you, Merry?"

Then she whispered, "I heard about your daddy. Are you sad?"

Shocked, he froze. But under her gaze, he slowly nodded.

She leaned forward and kissed his cheek. "My daddy says you'll be OK because you're a Quad-de. But if you need someone to cheer you up, you call me. Okay?"

Jake could only nod.

The ship soon joined the caravan heading toward Earth.

Ironically, after just 48-hours, Dr. Mangot was yelling at the infirmary nurses, "Let me out of here!"

Jake went to see her, feeling very much like a Quad-de who had to visit every sick person and cheer them up.

As soon as she saw Jake, Dr. Mangot demanded, "When do we leave?"

Jake explained that their ship was in use, which meant they'd have to wait for a return ship. Dr. Mangot seemed about to launch into a tirade. But Captain Bulmer touched her arm.

Something had changed between them. Jake didn't know when or exactly what, but between the two Phoke, there was a new awareness of each other. Their friendship had gone to a new place, and Jake was content to wait and see how it developed.

≈ ≈

While they waited for spaceships to return, Utz went looking for Kirkwall Rudak. He found him in the cafeteria during the early lunch shift. Utz took a deep breath, very aware that his body shape was so different from the Tizzalurians who dominated the room.

He stopped at Kirkwall's table and said politely. "Hello, I'm Utz Seehafer. I know your sister from Marasca University. May I talk to you?"

"Derry?" Kirkwall looked up hopefully. Then, his face fell, and he shook his head. "She's gone."

Of course, there was no privacy. But Utz forged ahead. "Um, no. I need to explain something. May I sit?"

Kirkwall's neighbor, another tall Tizzalurian, scooted over. Utz scrunched into the space. He hadn't thought to pick up his lunch yet, he had been so focused on talking to Kirkwall. So, it felt odd to have nothing before him. Utz straightened his shoulders and dove into the conversation.

"I met Derry at the university, and we became friends." Utz paused, looked up at the ceiling, and then determinedly looked at Kirkwall. "More than friends."

Kirkwall blinked and shrank away from Utz. "You're Bo-See?"

"I'm Risonian. That's all that will matter on Earth." Before his courage failed him, he blurted, "And I got Derry off-planet."

Kirkwall's face drained of color. "No. How? When?"

Utz began again. This was important because this man might become his brother-in-law. "I am Utz Seehafer, son of the late King Pharomond Seehafer." He choked up at the mention of his father, but forced himself to continue. "Derry and I became friends while we cared for some animals." He didn't want to explain about the great white sharks. That might come later, but not now. "My cousin is a smuggler."

Kirkwall's eyes were huge, and several people around them turned to stare.

Utz continued doggedly. "I had Derry smuggled to Earth."
"You did what?"

Utz nodded. "She'll be on Earth when we arrive."

One of the people at the table started clapping softly, and the whole table joined in.

One of them stood and called to the room. "His sister is safe! She got smuggled out."

Of course, the crowd didn't know Kirkwall or Derry or Utz. But it didn't matter. Any good news, any unexpected word that someone was safe—the entire room cheered.

Everyone stayed busy for the next few months while waiting to go home. They had to grow all their food, keep the moon in a stable orbit, organize evacuations, and keep the peace.

It would be a couple weeks before the big transports returned for more passengers. Jake and Blake busied themselves with helping organize people into groups to be ready for evacuation. Captain Bulmer's curiosity about Risonian pools led him to take charge of scheduling swim times. He also went with crews to check the pressurized water tanks at the far end of the Moon Base.

When a large spaceship returned, Blake and Jake helped everyone load, including Dr. Mangot and Captain Bulmer. They carried with them the starfish globes and would start research immediately.

But Blake and Jake waited for the next ship. And when it came, they waited again.

Waiting till the last transport was something that Swann would've done.

Jake told Blake to go back on an earlier flight, but Blake said, "No. If you're here, I'm here."

They bumped foreheads, and Jake acknowledged that Blake was right. He didn't want to be alone on the Cadee Moon Base, but he needed to stay. It was his way of saying: I'm a Quad-de.

They were on the last transport to leave the Cadee Moon Base. Cadee had become a tiny planetoid, circling in a perfect orbit around Turco.

QUARANTINED

Jake, Blake, and Utz disembarked at the Altai Space Port in southwestern Mongolia on March 15, the last evacuees from the Cadee Moon Base. Upon exiting, they were directed to a room to be fitted with cold weather clothing. Jumpsuits, thin-but-very-warm coats made from high-tech materials, sturdy boots, gloves and a cap. Because so many Tizzalurians were tall, the selection of clothing was good for Jake and Dad. Utz had a harder time with his squat, short figure, but finally they were all outfitted.

They had to wait a couple hours, but at least the room had large windows overlooking the mountain valley. A couple of small buildings marked the entrance to the underground colony that had been hastily renovated for the Risonians. The pale winter sun did nothing to relieve the frigid winter air. This Chinese installation was actually in Southwestern Mongolia, which was a barren land with seemingly desert areas where the only thing green was a few shrubs or perhaps lichen on a rock. Mountains in the distance were capped with white—snow, clouds, or both. It rarely snowed or rained in the winter months. Only the summers were wet—and that, only moderately wet.

It was a cruel quarantine for the Risonians. Arid. Dry. Thousands of miles from water. The Khazkan River ran near the city of Altai, but the local Mongolians were fiercely protective of it. In their orientation session, officials warned the Risonians not to go near it, or they'd be arrested. The river drained into the Lake Khyargas, but it was a salt lake. The smaller freshwater Airag Lake might be tempting, but it was within the protected Khyargas Lake National Park, which was strictly forbidden.

Effectively, the Risonians were confined within an arid landscape. So, they fled underground, where tunnel air was treated with humidifiers. Still dry, but it brought the humidity up to barely livable levels. The swimming pools were popular, of course. But the three pools were constantly booked. And frankly, they weren't adequately filtered and refreshed with clean water often enough, so they became stale. All in all, an unhappy place for the Risonians.

Finally, the crew from Cadee was allowed to exit the holding area. First, there was a receiving line, and Jake willed himself to be calm while they shook each and every person's hand. Jake chafed at the formality, which did nothing but cause delays. Mom stood last in the line of officials. He wanted to hug her, but in her ambassadorial role, she was too formal and wouldn't allow it.

"Later," she murmured. "We'll have all the time on Earth we need."

"Okay, later," he said. Then he had to ask: "Is Em here?"

Mom shook her head, "No. She's volunteering at something because we had no idea when they'd release you. I sent her a message, though, so she's coming now."

"I have something for you," Jake said, refusing to wait for a more private moment like Mom wanted. From his backpack, he pulled out a small wrapped gift and handed to her.

She looked at him quizzically before she ripped off the bright paper and pulled open the box. Inside, there was tissue paper to push aside before she saw it.

"Oh!"

She pulled out the photo that Jake had taken from Swann's desk, the one of the three of them on a picnic. It showed Dayexi laughing up at Swann, who hugged an eight-year-old Jake.

Now, ambassador or not, Mom pulled Jake into a hug, and clung to him. "Did he—?"

Jake knew she was asking about Swann, but he had nothing to give her. At the end, he hadn't asked about her, or sent any last word.

He just shook his head.

Mom pushed away, squared her shoulders and nodded. But she clutched the box with the photo, and Jake knew it would find a place on her ambassador's desk, a memory of happier times.

Utz slapped him on the shoulder. "We made it."

Jake introduced his mother. "Have you met Ambassador Dayexi Quad-de?"

"A pleasure."

But Utz was barely paying attention. Instead, something caught his eye. Across the crowd, a tall man—Kirkwall!—waved at them. Standing beside him was his sister, Derry.

Without another glance at the ambassador, Utz trotted to them and scooped up Derry, twirling around and around. She squealed but held him tight when he set her down a moment later. He bent to kiss her, and when he looked up, he looked dazed like his world had just changed.

Jake knew that feeling! That poor Bo-See has going to have an interesting life if he'd chosen a Tizzalurian woman.

A pang of loneliness struck him, though. Utz and Derry were together, but he was still alone. Again, Jake swept the crowd in search of Em. She still wasn't here.

The wide-open reception room was cold. Mom stepped up to the podium, and in her Ambassador role, gave a short speech about the bravery of those who had remained behind at the Cadee Moon Base and been the last to evacuate.

Jake barely listened. He searched the faces of every single female there. Still no Em. Disappointment stung him. He thought back to that long-ago day when he'd first seen her at the coffee shop on Bainbridge. That was before the rogue EL-LIS forces tried to sabotage Mt. Rainier, and before they knew Em was a Phoke with family that lived in Aberforth Hills in the North Sea. It was before he went back to Rison for a frantic search and a poignant good-bye. So much had happened; so much had changed.

Even that first day, Jake had known that Em was special. Where was she?

Polite applause brought him back to the present. He shivered, but he didn't know if it was from the cold or from worry about Em.

The group of people broke apart. Dad had his arm draped across Mom's shoulder, and they strolled toward him. She stopped him, though, and Dad leaned over to listen to something she said. He looked up startled. "No. Not possible."

Mom grinned and nodded. "Yes."

Jake strode to them and asked. "What?"

"Are you telling everyone?" Dad shrugged. "Do you want Jake to know now?"

Rolling his eye, Jake said, "You have to tell me now."

Mom's grin got even bigger. "Yes. But you'll understand when I say that this can't be shared outside the family."

Jake nodded and waited.

"I'm expecting. You'll soon have a brother or sister."

Shock sent a shiver over Jake. "Wait. Is this another test tube experiment?"

Mom sobered and Dad slipped his arm back around her shoulder. "No. Not a test tube."

Jake was stunned. It meant that Risonians could marry Earthlings. It meant—

"Jake!"

From across the room, he saw her.

Her face was red and chapped from the cold outside, as red as the cap she wore.

Em.

His heart gave a funny leap. Her thick jacket was unzipped, revealing a black shirt underneath. And gleaming against the black was the amber mermaid necklace. She still wore it. Even under all the winter gear, he could tell that she was thinner, but her smile was as brilliant as ever.

My siren, he thought with satisfaction. At times on this long trip, he'd wondered if he had just dreamed her.

He pulled a gift for her out of his backpack, and hid it behind his back. He couldn't take his eyes off her as they walked toward each other.

Em took off the cap and stuffed it into a pocket. Her dark hair was full of static electricity in the dry air, and it stuck up randomly.

When they were a pace apart, he brought the gift from behind his back. It was a paper rose, a tiny origami masterpiece, made for Jake by one of the other engineers who'd stayed behind on Cadee.

"A rose from Jake Rose."

Her delighted laughter lifted his spirits even more.

"And something else," he said. Shyly, he pulled a Valentine from his coat pocket. While traveling back to Earth, Valentine's Day had come and gone. He'd had little else to do, so he'd made five Valentines. Dad, Utz and the other passengers voted on which one to keep.

"Keep it funny," the engineer had told him.

The sappy sweet one lost. The too casual, just-friends Valentine was the worst rated. The winner had an attempt at humor, the best he could manage because Earth humor was still difficult for him. He still went back and forth about giving it to her since Valentine's Day was a month ago, but he decided that something was better than nothing.

Em pulled the Valentine out of the envelope. He had handcut a red paper heart and typed the words in a fancy script.

Em read, "You're the best thing alive!" She looked up, puzzled, obviously wondering what the inside would say. Slowly, she turned the page and read, "Except for *wolkev*. And they're extinct."

She giggled. "You do like your *wolkev*."

Jake beamed. Getting a small laugh was a triumph—as always. "I've got one growing in a pot!" he said. "When they release it from quarantine, you'll see it."

"How long till it's big enough to have fruit?" Em asked.

Jake thought about his brief stay on Earth. A moment from a history class with Coach Blevins came back to him. They were talking about the Pilgrims, the first European settlers of America. Coach quoted one of the Pilgrim leaders who said, "We knew we were Pilgrims."

All the Risonians gathered here in the desert compound, they knew that they were Pilgrims. They had come to a new planet to start fresh, to find new ways of embracing life.

"Five years till the *wolkevs* have fruit," he told Em.

Soberly, she said, "We may still be here at Altai in five years."

"You're right. But eventually, they'll have to share Earth with us. We're here, not there. And that changes everything."

Em took his hand and pulled him over to a large window. "Look. They have beautiful sunsets here."

But Jake looked at her instead, with a glad heart. They'd been born a galaxy apart, and yet here they were together. Life was indeed a journey, a pilgrimage of the heart.

And he bent to kiss her.

ABOUT THE AUTHOR

Translated into nine languages, children's book author **DARCY PATTISON** writes picture books, middle grade novels, and children's nonfiction. Her work has been recognized by *starred reviews* in *Kirkus*, *BCCB*, and *PW*.

Three books have been named National Science Teachers Association Outstanding Science Trade Books: *Desert Baths* (2013); *Abayomi, the Brazilian Puma* (2015), and *Nefertiti, the Spidernaut* (2017).

The Nantucket Sea Monster: A Fake News Story is a December 2017 Junior Library Guild selection. She is a member of the Society of Children's Bookwriters and Illustrators and the Author's Guild. For more information, see

darcypattison.com/about OR mimshouse.com

Join our mailing list: MimsHouse.com/newsletter/

THE BLUE PLANETS WORLD SERIES
Envoys (Prequel – short story)
Sleepers (Book 1)
Sirens (Book 2)
Pilgrims (Book 3)

OTHER NOVELS BY DARCY PATTISON
Saucy and Bubba: A Hansel and Gretel Tale
The Girl, the Gypsy and the Gargyole
Vagabonds
Liberty
Longing for Normal

The Aliens, Inc. Series – short chapter books
   Book 1: Kell, the Alien
   Book 2: Kell and the Horse Apple Parade
   Book 3: Kell and the Giants
   Book 4: Kell and the Detectives

PILGRIMS

92317191R00104

Made in the USA
Middletown, DE
07 October 2018